LIQUID
SHADES
OF BLUE

LIQUID SHADES OF BLUE

A NOVEL

JAMES POLKINGHORN

OCEANVIEW PUBLISHING

SARASOTA, FLORIDA

ISBN 978-1-60809-616-9

Published in the United States of America by Oceanview Publishing

Sarasota, Florida

www.oceanviewpub.com

10 9 8 7 6 5 4 3 2

To my mother, Janet Clark
". . . who sang like a lark, in the park, when it's dark."

ACKNOWLEDGMENTS

This book would not have found its way into print without the selfless efforts of Michael Connelly, who provided invaluable substantive advice and insight.

Larry Loftis encouraged me from the start and kept my spirits up when they were flagging.

Thanks to Bob and Pat Gussin and the Oceanview staff for their enthusiastic support.

LIQUID SHADES OF BLUE

PROLOGUE

She glanced at the eight pills in her hand and the glass of water on the finely carved cherrywood dressing table before her. She looked up.

"I hate pain. I can't handle it."

"So, swallow the pills," he said. "You'll feel nothing. It will be like going to sleep."

A pause. She considered his words, her situation, and the note she had written. She reached for the glass.

CHAPTER ONE

The day began badly but the worst was coming. This is the way of many stories, although I hadn't thought of it in a comparative way until I began piecing this together. It's been a while since it all happened. You wonder about the effect of traumatic events on already imperfect memory and about perceived connections that may not even be real. You, at least, understand that I'm alive to tell this tale, if that's what it turns out to be. But what of the damage done? What's the result of all that?

There I was, opening my eyes uncertainly, head throbbing and lips dry; definitely a hangover—nothing new. A shaft of light from a nearby window revealed the murky outline of furniture I recognized as my own. *Safe in my own bed at least*, I fleetingly thought. But then I heard the soft breathing that was clearly not mine. Turning slowly—agonizingly—to my left, I encountered the bare shoulder and silky black hair of Anna Markova, a high-end Key West sex worker I knew casually from her sporadic visits to my bar.

"Good Lord, Jack! What have you done?" I whispered.

I was dully transfixed by a small heart tattoo on her shoulder blade, wondering why she put it there where she would never see it. I noticed a light dusting of freckles on her otherwise alabaster

skin, offering proof that she did sometimes venture out in the tropical Key West sun, although I had only seen her in artificial light.
I pondered these things while my mind otherwise raced to fill the
void that was last night. Needing answers, I lightly squeezed her
right shoulder and watched as she slowly but fluidly rolled over to
face me. Her startling cornflower blue eyes settled on me. I tried
to hold her gaze but peripherally saw that she was naked, at least
from the waist up. As she reached forward to touch my cheek with
the back of her hand, she made no effort to adjust the sheet that
partially covered us.

"Good morning, Jack. How are you feeling?"

"Never better, Anna. Why are we here?"

She smiled, revealing perfect white teeth and soft lips made to
be kissed.

"You don't remember, Jack? I think I should take this moment
to be insulted. Most men find me memorable."

Her small, firm breasts and seemingly erect nipples taunted me.
Still nothing.

"Did we . . ."

"No, Jack. I think it was not the right time. Maybe never the
right time."

Her breath smelled like orange blossoms. I was certain mine
did not. Still foggy, I pressed on.

"So how did you . . . or should I say we . . . end up here?"

"Such an interesting question, Jack, if you stand back from it
a little bit. But I think you are looking for a simple answer, yes?"

"Please, Anna, give me a little bit of a break. I'm struggling
here." My voice sounded scratchy and weak. Hers rang clearly,
natural seduction in every accented word.

"It really is simple. I am not teasing you. It is late Friday night
and I am without arrangement, which is not so usual this time of

year. I am walking along Duval Street and I notice your new sign down the alley. I really do like it. 'Jack's Hideaway.' Very good description and also says something personal about you, I think."

She paused—I didn't bite. I looked back as steadily as I could, not knowing what I told her in the hours before. She continued.

"I just stop in to see how things are going. You and Tracy are behind the bar, most stools are taken, and the tables are full. I sit at the bar in front by the window. I am watching you in the mirror behind the bar. I know you know I am there, but you don't look at me, which makes me smile. It is dim and the music is loud enough to make people speak up. They are less, what you call, self-conscious. But not you, Jack. You have been here almost two years, and I never see you speaking with pretty girls. Or pretty boys either. But I know your eyes are on me when I come in just for that second of recognizing. You have been watching me, but I confess. I have been watching you too."

Now this was interesting. It's true that I had picked up a six-year sub-lease on the bar known as Billy & Bob's. Both Billy and Bob lived in Ohio and never noticed until it was too late that their manager/nephew was stealing from them. He had some ideas about investing in a human smuggling operation focused on Cuba but was too dumb to realize that everyone he was trying to con-spire with was an FBI agent or informant. He's in prison now, and I took advantage of his uncles' disgust and financial problem by buying their business, struggling though it was, and taking over their lease. I finally changed the name about six months ago when I realized we were going to make it. Investing in the locals was the key, and after enough of them got to know me, it made sense to put my own name on the place.

We're a little off the main drag in Old Town, but you can see us from there. People living on the little lanes between Duval and

Whitehead Streets, along with the working-class folks living in Bahama Village, needed a place they could walk to, enjoy a stiff drink at a fair price, and talk to their friends without being bowled over by a drunk stockbroker looking for another Jager shot for "his bros" from New Jersey. I made it a point to remember names of repeat customers and Tracy, my tireless lead bartender who was there from the start, had developed a couple of rum cocktails that were gaining a fearsome reputation by word of mouth.

Anna would appear every couple of months, as I remembered it, usually alone but sometimes with men and women I came to realize were clients rather than friends. A six-foot stunner, most conversations paused when she came into view. I guess it's true that I kept an eye on her, but I preferred to think it was because I wanted to make sure she wasn't conducting business in my place. I was still new and still trying to understand how the local police viewed the wide gray line between acceptable and arrestable behavior. In Key West, we don't think so much about whether conduct is illegal—it's more about who's being hurt. Personally, I had no problem with sex workers making a living, but I also knew that professionals like Anna held secrets that could hurt people I wasn't ready to cross.

"Anna, forgive me, but my brain isn't really working. I'm still not remembering what happened, although you don't seem to be mad at me."

"Not a bit, Jack. You are a perfect gentleman, even after too much vodka."

Except I don't really drink vodka, at least not as a first choice. But if I did, it would explain my current condition. I tried to lift my head off the pillow but immediately regretted it.

"So how did vodka come into it?"

"Well, you are avoiding me as always until the drunk Navy guy is getting pushy with me—not accepting that I am not interested.

I get up to leave, but he blocks my way. He is making a scene, which is bad for me. I just want to go. And then suddenly you are there."

And then I remembered.

He had grabbed her arm as she tried to slip past him to the door, which violated one of the cardinal rules of Jack's Hideaway: no one touches a woman who doesn't want to be touched. That brought me out from behind the bar in an instant. I simultaneously peeled his fingers from Anna's arm and pulled his hand behind his back while pushing him forward into the bar with my free forearm. I had the benefit of not being drunk, so, for him, this all happened too fast. With his face now pressed into the bar-top wet with beer spilled during the commotion, I told him he was going to apologize, I was going to let him up, and he was going to leave, in that order.

Luckily, his three friends made no effort to intervene. One of them, wearing a blue "Fly Navy" baseball cap, leaned in and said, "Let's go, Zeke, we've got the training run in the morning anyway."

I added, "Listen to me, Zeke. That run will not be pleasant with the broken nose I'm about to administer if you try to fight me. Got it?"

Zeke seemed to be considering his options, but I noticed he was no longer straining to free his arm from my grip. This was over.

"So now I need that apology, Zeke."

He spat out the word "sorry" as I slowly eased him upright, shoving him toward his friends, who wisely reached out to prevent him from doing anything impulsive.

"Don't bring him back here."

The Key West Naval Air Station, located about four miles down the road on Boca Chica Key, is a big employer and provider of many drinking customers to bars like mine. It's home to several service units, including Fighter Squadron Composite 111, an air-to-air combat training group of both active and reserve duty pilots with significant combat experience. The squadron is known as the Sun Downers, taken from the famous F-14 Tomcat Squadron from Miramar, California, disestablished by the Navy in 1995.

The Key West Sun Downers understand their traditions. They are deadly serious in the air and, in my experience, come in two types on the ground. The first group—a large majority—are calm, affable, intelligent, and possessed of a quiet confidence that doesn't require demonstration. The second group is cocky, loud, and determined to one-up anyone in any competition and in any context. My new friend Zeke was in the second group, but his friends were in the first and quickly walked him out as I considered whether this incident was going to hurt my reputation on Boca Chica.

Only then did I turn to see that the place was back to normal, glasses clinking and voices rising, except that Anna stood very still by the bar squeezing her fists so tightly I could see the veins bulging on the backs of her hands. Her eyes were fixed on the four pilots as they pushed out the door. Her expression was hard to read. Disgust? Contempt? But for whom? She felt me watching her and the spell was broken. The remarkable geometry of her face—the angular cheekbones, aquiline nose, and strong Slavic jawline—took on an appearance of diffidence, something I'd never seen in Anna before.

"I know I must say thank you, Jack, but I want you to know I can take care of myself. That man would not harm me."

And, with that statement, her confidence returned. She crossed her arms over her chest and took a half-step forward. I had the awkward feeling of knowing the next thing I said was likely to be wrong. I started with, "I'm sorry, Anna. I simply reacted and wasn't thinking. I didn't mean to embarrass you."

This elicited a smile, which seemed promising.

"I am not embarrassed, Jack. This is too strong a word. But I do not need to be protected from men like him by men like you. I know you are the big strong type that wants to protect, but I do not need this."

"That's not quite it, Anna. I wasn't so much trying to protect you as I was trying to educate him on the rules of respect. I don't like bullies. I react badly to people who think they can have what they want by being bigger, stronger, or louder than the next person. Zeke needed some pretty basic instruction in terms he understood."

Anna appraised me for a moment before speaking again.

"Then I congratulate you, Jack. You are a first-rate instructor, even though I do not understand how you control Zeke so quickly. I will buy you a drink to toast your success."

And before I could respond, she turned and ordered two shots of Grey Goose vodka from Tracy, who by this time had drifted down to our spot at the bar. She was carrying her cell phone, seemingly poised to dial 911 if things had turned a different way. Although Tracy is only five feet two inches in height and couldn't weigh more than a hundred and ten pounds, her presence is palpable. People notice when she's around, even before they see her mane of unruly red hair and unusual beryl green eyes set wide in an expression of perpetual amusement. I'd guess she's a few years older than me, possibly thirty-three or thirty-four. Now she was clearly not amused and stared at me intently as if she had not heard Anna speak. I nodded silently and watched her turn to pull the bottle from the shelf below the register, noting the force with which she then slammed the two shot glasses on the bar top, startling a smiling young couple enjoying rum drinks nearby. She poured the shots without a word and left the bottle on the bar as she stalked off in her lithe, cat-like way.

"I don't think she likes me, Jack."

"I don't think it's you, Anna. She just hates drama, particularly after midnight."

"She might be in wrong business in wrong town."

"She might not disagree except she has a gift for mixing cocktails, and people like talking to her. The bad drunks are the problem, so I usually try not to schedule her to close the place. I needed her tonight, though, and now she's pissed. No worries, Anna."

"Very well then," she said as she picked up her glass. "*Na Zdorovie*, Jack. I am glad we are speaking."

"Cheers, Anna. I'm glad we're speaking too."

With that, we knocked down our shots, neither of us giving any sign of the inevitable burning at the back of the throat when the first shot goes down. I smiled and asked, "Why is a Russian woman like you not ordering Russian vodka? Aren't there rules about that?"

She did not smile back.

"Russia has nothing for me, Jack. Nothing!"

There was some venom in that last word.

So that's how it started. I was now peering through the remaining fog in my mind, trying to remember the rest of it as Anna looked at me calmly, her face expressionless. I remembered sitting at the bar as the customers began to leave and Tracy went through the closing procedure, periodically looking over to see what I was doing. Which was talking to a person I was feeling strangely connected to. There was more drinking and more talking, but I realized, in memory, that I was the one doing most of both. That was unusual. I remembered Tracy leaving and ordering me to lock up when I left. I remembered Anna taking me by the hand and walking me toward the back door through the storeroom, which led to a courtyard and the converted garage where I had been living since closing on the place. I remembered standing at the door of the apartment and struggling to open it. Anna placed her hand over mine to steady it and it felt like electricity. I remembered that. We were then very close, noses touching, but I knew I was fading. And so did she, judging by the bemused smile on her face. The rest of it eluded me, hidden in blackness.

And then my cell phone rang from the nightstand beside me, pulling me from the dark murk of recollection.

CHAPTER TWO

I turned and seized the phone like it was a live grenade, hit DISMISS, and rolled back toward Anna, dropping the phone on the bed between us. Anna was impassive.

"You do not even look to see who is calling you so early on Saturday morning, Jack. Maybe it is important."

"I don't think I can do anything important right now, Anna. I'll call back later, whoever it is."

I buried my face in the pillow. But then the phone exploded again, between us. This time Anna deftly snatched it from the sheet, glanced at it quickly, and thrust it toward me.

"You must answer this."

Without strength to argue, I blindly took the phone, swiped at the green spot, and pressed it to my ear. I croaked out the word "hello."

"Good morning, Jack. It's the Duke."

This was a voice I had not heard directly since I moved to Key West: my father, Claude "Duke" Girard, referring to himself in the third person, as was his custom.

"Something has happened, and I wanted you to hear it from me first. There might be some press coverage, and I don't know who you're in touch with these days."

There was rebuke in this. I felt my heart rate accelerate as I prepared to engage, but he pressed on.

"Your mother is dead, Jack. She committed suicide. A drug overdose. Valium and alcohol according to the initial tox screen."

No words formed. I was quite literally speechless, and I felt sweat breaking out on my forehead. From the corner of my eye, I saw that Anna was moving. She slipped out of bed and glided across the tile to the chair by the bedroom door where she apparently left her dress. Picking it up, she turned, naked and unabashed, to blow me a kiss, concern reflected in her eyes.

Without hesitating, she turned again and padded through the doorway to the living room, closing the door behind her. Less than a minute later, I heard the front door open and close and she was gone. There was an erotic and confusing quality to this escape, but I couldn't linger on it.

"Jack! Are you there? I know this is a shock."

I was still not connecting his words to any sort of recognizable reality. My mind was a jumble of cascading images I couldn't make out clearly. I considered the possibility that none of this was real. But I heard my father's impatient breathing and knew I must somehow speak.

"When?" was all I could muster. My heart was beating so hard I could feel it thumping against the bedsheet.

"Apparently, it's been three or four days. They don't know for sure. The housekeeper at the condo found her yesterday morning and called 911. The police got me on my cell around noon."

"And you're just calling me now."

It was an observation rather than a question.

"Don't get sensitive, Son. With the divorce going on, I had to find out what the hell actually happened and figure out how to handle it. All I knew was that she was dead and that it looked like a suicide. Those ratfuckers from the *Herald* and Channel 7 would be straight up my ass with insinuations if someone didn't take control of this and make sure the suicide part of it was clear-cut. That had to be the first thing out when the story leaked. So, I went over there to sort it out."

"No doubt you did."

At the time, my father was a prominent, some might say infamous, Miami trial lawyer who had seized upon the loosening of lawyer advertising rules back in the nineties to launch one of the first systematic television advertising campaigns. Tall and handsome in his dark, Gallic way, with a military bearing honed during his service in Army military intelligence during the Gulf War, he had a knack for establishing visceral connections to people desperate for salvation in the worst circumstances of their lives—all through the flat-screened boxes in their living rooms. At first, he solicited any type of personal injury claim, but he soon shrewdly observed the influence of insurance on the practice of medicine and began targeting victims of medical malpractice. At the same time, pharmaceutical companies were pumping out new drugs and advertising them directly to the public, generating never-before-seen profits and a second group of preferred clients for Duke Girard & Associates: victims of prescription drugs in some form or fashion.

Once he focused on these two groups of people, business boomed, and his practice expanded to include five to ten highly paid lawyers and ten to fifteen paralegals who did the preliminary screening of cases and most of the unglamorous investigation and gathering of information for the cases deemed acceptable. The money train never would have gotten rolling without courtroom success, though, and that was where the Duke was unmatched. He did two things naturally that most lawyers can't learn to do however hard they try. First, he could tell a simple and compelling story that jurors felt rather than thought about, no matter how complex the facts. Second, he could "de-select" a jury with laser-like precision, the most underrated skill in the trial lawyer's arsenal.

Most lawyers focus their attention on "selecting" the best jurors from the available panel, using the limited challenges assigned by the judge. The Duke, on the other hand, focused on identifying and eliminating the specific potential jurors who not only would be hostile to his claim, but would effectively advocate that hostility to the other jurors once they were left alone. With those jurors off the case, the Duke had ultimate confidence in his ability to reach the others, fixing them one by one with his seemingly bottomless black eyes as he sang his tale of pain and woe in his mellifluous baritone. Men and women alike were helplessly attracted to him and hung on every word. A string of multimillion-dollar verdicts followed, and before long the insurance and drug companies were voluntarily disgorging a rising percentage of their ever-increasing profits to settle cases and avoid meeting the Duke in the courtroom.

Wealth followed, and in Miami wealth is power. Which brought the Duke to the condominium overlooking Government Cut on South Beach to "sort out" the circumstances of my mother's death and ensure that when the police inevitably leaked the story to their press contacts, the tragedy would be revealed as a self-inflicted loss of life and nothing more.

But I wasn't thinking that all the way through as I struggled to comprehend what my father was telling me. I was numbly wondering why I wasn't feeling more emotion. *Am I in shock? What's wrong with me?*

"So, I think I've got it under control, Jack, but you need to get here today. I don't want the press assholes talking to you before we've talked things over face-to-face. A lot has happened in two years. Plus, there's the thing about your brother."

That straightened me up.

"What does Bobby have to do with this?"

"Don't be naïve. That connection just multiplies the tragedy, and they're going to ask you about all of it. You're still a lawyer. Think about it logically."

"I can't think about anything right now . . . Dad. And you're the last person in the world I want to talk to about the law. Listen, I'm hanging up now. I'll be there as soon as I can."

With that, the call ended. I sagged back against the pillows and pulled the covers up to my chin, staring vacantly at the ceiling, waiting to feel something.

CHAPTER THREE

The 160-mile drive from Key West to Miami on the mostly two-laned Overseas Highway takes three and a half to four and a half hours on a Saturday in January owing mostly to the prevailing 45 mph speed limit and the typically miserable traffic in now overdeveloped Islamorada. There are only so many cars to be packed onto the single-file road there, and when droves of tourists are added to the usual crowd of locals moving about doing Saturday chores or trying to get their boats in the water, the result feels a little like a weekday rush hour in Manhattan.

And so it was with this prospect that I set out from Key West later in the morning. Although numb and hungover, I had managed to pull myself out of bed and take a steaming hot shower to elicit some sensation. Operating on a sort of autopilot afterward, I called Tracy and told her I had a family emergency and would have to go to Miami for a few days. For some reason I couldn't just tell her that my mother was dead, possibly because it wasn't real for me yet. Regardless, I put her in charge and made sure she was ready for Reggae Sunday, the very popular rum-soaked party we threw every week featuring live music from two local bands. I also called the Key West Track & Field Club to ask forgiveness for not being able to participate in the remainder of the Pole Vault in

Paradise event going on that weekend. The annual competition invites elite club vaulters from around the country to enjoy a few days in Key West while helping to raise money for the Key West High School Track and Field Team. As a former decathlete in college, I took pride in the event and participated both as a sponsor and competitor the last two years. I was due to jump later in the afternoon but now had to bow out, which, in my current condition, was no great loss to the competition.

Cruising north, away from Stock Island just outside of Key West, I realized I hadn't eaten and so turned right on Boca Chica Road and rumbled along the poorly paved surface past mangroves and stilt houses until reaching the small sign directing me left to Geiger Key Marina. I parked my beat-up but reliable black 1978 Jeep CJ7 in the lot and made my way over to the rustic, thatch-roofed building that housed the open-air bar and restaurant. Seating myself at the bar, I gazed out at the wind-whipped water flowing between the small mangrove hammocks and wondered again at the beauty of it all. The sun was shining directly on the shallows, revealing a kaleidoscope of blue, green, yellow, and brown as the current surged over the sea grass bottom.

"You look like shit, Jack."

"Back at ya, Patrick."

I turned to see the concerned expression on the thin, timeworn face of Patrick Lonagan, a longtime Key West bartender who, at this late stage of his career, was working day shifts off the island.

"Shee-it, Jack! I always look this way. You're the one who drew every female eye the minute you showed up at Billy & Bob's. All blue eyes and blond hair and . . . Listen to me!"

After an embarrassed pause, he added, "What's happened, Jack? Are you sick?"

"Probably a little, but that's not it. It seems that my . . . well, let me just say that I got some bad news that has me heading back to Miami."

"Not permanently!"

"No, no. I'll definitely be back. This is home now."

As I said it, I realized I really meant it, possibly only just then feeling the conviction of those words. Where I was heading was not home anymore, but something else entirely.

"Well, let me get you a cold beer and a fried hogfish sandwich. The boys brought in four big hogfish from up past Cape Sable a couple of hours ago."

I realized I was starving.

"That sounds perfect, Patrick. Make it a Coors Light. I have some driving ahead of me. And go ahead and put the cheese, onions, and peppers on the fish."

Because it's light and sweet, hogfish is delicious any way it's prepared, but adding American cheese with sautéed onions and green peppers as they do at Geiger Key Marina creates an unmatched taste sensation. It's an explosion of flavor and texture with each bite.

"Will do, Jack. And here's your beer."

He pulled the can from the ice barrel and set it in front of me with the mountains on the front a very bright blue. I cracked it open and took a long swallow as Patrick turned back to the kitchen. Looking out toward the water again, my mind began sifting impressions, thoughts, and memories without landing on anything in particular. My mother was dead, but I couldn't really see her. It was all moving too fast and I was unable to fix on any image or feeling. Eventually, Patrick broke my apparent reverie.

"Here's your sandwich. On the house. I really hope things go your way in Miami this time."

"Thanks, Patrick, but this time it's not about me."

CHAPTER FOUR

Back in the Jeep trundling north in a long line of vehicles of all descriptions, I popped my Bob Marley *Legend* CD into the disc changer and allowed my mind to drift as I passed through the Lower Keys. This compilation record had been a source of great comfort to me in periods of stress in my life, and I turned to it now as I tried once again to settle on some way of feeling about the loss of my mother.

Betty Evangeline Donovan Girard was born into old Miami money in 1966 and came of age in the eighties, a particularly tumultuous time in the city, marked by the Mariel boatlift, "white flight," large-scale drug running, and the birth of South Beach as a hedonist mecca. But families like the Donovans were as deeply rooted as the banyan trees forming the spectacular canopies over their quiet Coral Gables streets. They were built to weather any storm. And did.

As a Donovan, Betty grew up at Riviera Country Club and the Coral Reef Yacht Club, instructed in golf, tennis, and sailing. Tall and athletic all her life, excellence came easily to her, but her passion was never in sports. It wasn't in academics either, although she earned good grades at the private schools she attended with a carefree attitude that irritated her instructors. Instead, Betty's passion was for living. Endlessly curious about people and places, she sought new experiences wherever she could find them. She was drawn to artists and musicians, fascinated by the ability of some lucky few to move people's emotions by expressing their own. As an only child in a wealthy and powerful family, her exuberance was interpreted as rebelliousness, leading to clashes, discipline, acting out, and more discipline. I've never known the details of my mother's adolescent life, but a combination of events, inclinations, and acquaintances led her to casual experimentation with alcohol and drugs. Pot and ecstasy were in vogue, but cocaine was literally washing up on the beaches in Miami, making it both cheap and easy to get.

And Betty liked it.

Under its influence, her already outgoing personality was magnified by ten. I didn't know it until much later, but Betty's drug use got her expelled from one high school before she graduated from another. This wrecked her chance to follow the Donovan path to the Ivy League and led to her admission at the public, but respectable, University of Florida. This was where she encountered the Duke, changing everything.

The thought of my father snapped me back to the more recent past, particularly the last year, when my mother broke ranks and filed for divorce. I was already in Key West at the time, having made my own escape the year before. My relationship with my mother had always been complicated and I had no interest in involving myself in a drama I knew was multifaceted. I believed she had sided with the Duke one too many times on things that mattered. To me, anyway. I had also experienced her deep disappointment in me and was still stinging from the bitterness of her rebuke not so long ago. So I avoided her calls and responded to texts with terse, emotionless updates. But what was she feeling during that year that led to this? How did the pain become unbearable? Was there really no one for her to turn to?

My ignorance was a heavy burden. As I rolled through Layton, my guilt pressed harder and harder on my still-clouded mind. From the narrow ribbon of roadway dividing the Gulf of Mexico and the Atlantic Ocean, I saw shimmering liquid shades of blue to the left and right. As Bob Marley struck the opening acoustic notes of "Redemption Song," I finally felt the first tears trickling from the corners of my eyes. Thus released, with shoulders heaving, I silently wept.

CHAPTER FIVE

Leaving Key Largo behind and entering the desolate eighteen-mile stretch of U.S. 1 connecting the Florida Keys to the mainland, my thoughts began to circle around the eerie fact that two of the four members of my immediate family had taken their own lives by drug overdose. In 2009, at age twenty-one, my brother, Bobby, died of an oxycodone overdose shortly after graduating from the University of Florida with a Fine Arts degree. The death was initially reported as a tragic accident consistent with the rampant misuse of opioid drugs so freely prescribed for any ache or pain at the time. The Duke ensured that it stayed that way, exerting influence 360 miles north of Miami in Gainesville, where the body was found in the condominium Bobby shared. The investigation was brief; the scene was consistent with an accidental death in large part because there was no note or other evidence of intentional homicide. But I knew differently because I was the one who shared the condominium and found the body. And the note.

Robert Kennedy Girard was conceived in the aftermath of a fraternity graduation party in May 1987. The Duke and my mother, Betty, had been dating for a couple of years, although not always exclusively. Betty was an English major focusing on 20th Century American Literature and dabbled as a painter. Refining her attitude as a free thinker, she enjoyed deep conversations about philosophical topics she encountered in her reading and was attracted to intellectuals who opened her eyes to new ideas. The problem for Betty was that she wasn't often physically attracted to these deep thinkers. As she told me years later, that was where cocaine stepped in, making every potentially dull encounter dramatically more exciting.

But with the Duke she required no external stimulation. Blond and fair-skinned with bright cerulean blue eyes, she was the physical opposite of the Duke with his swarthy coloring, simmering black eyes, and tousled mane of dark hair. Their chemical attraction was instant, and Betty was overwhelmed by his singular masculinity. She fought it, though, because she still believed that human attraction could be rationally controlled, and that intellectual compatibility was the best foundation for a successful relationship. Ultimately, she lost the fight.

Of course, the Duke was no dummy, but his intellect revealed itself in ways Betty found unsettling. He had grown up as the youngest of three boys in an upper-middle-class family in Winter Park, Florida, a leafy and affluent suburb of Orlando. His father, an insurance broker, proudly traced the family's lineage to the exodus from France of aristocratic Protestant Huguenots suddenly persecuted after the Revocation of the Edict of Nantes by devoutly Catholic Louis XIV in 1685. Many of these expatriates settled in the South, including the Girards. Young Claude Girard, generations later, possessed a regal bearing from an early age, at least in the eyes of his wistful father, earning him the nickname "Duke." Claude was naturally happy to trade his given name for his nickname and set about living up to it in whatever his life was to become. Gifted in language, he learned to speak Spanish fluently through interaction with the family's live-in housekeeper,

Rosa. He picked up French at the behest of his father before leaving high school, and he could make his way around in Creole after working with Haitian migrant workers during the annual Central Florida citrus harvest. The Girards believed in the ameliorative effect of labor, a belief the Duke eventually brought with him to our family.

Upon reaching college, the Duke became a psychology major with a minor in Arabic, an odd combination to say the least but one right in line with his natural gifts. He got a kick out of describing the neuroses and personality disorders driving the transparent attempts of Betty's several other suitors to seduce her while they feigned interest in her intellectual and artistic talents. His apparent lack of jealousy bothered her, as if he knew he would win out in the end or, more frustratingly, didn't much care one way or the other. This went on right up to graduation, by which point the Duke had been successfully wooed by Army recruiters, who had been keeping an eye on him ever since he showed a real aptitude for Arabic. This was apparently going on at universities all over the country at the time. My mother never admitted this, but my suspicion came to be that she intentionally became pregnant with Bobby just as the Duke was moving to who knew where in order to keep him in her life. I don't think she expected marriage, but she hoped to keep their connection alive.

The Duke was another drug, and Betty was hooked.

If the Duke ever shared my suspicion, he never let on and instead proposed to Betty and arranged a civil ceremony to take place just as he was leaving for basic training. I think he liked the idea of marrying into the Donovan family and believed he could eventually smooth over the aggravation of Betty's parents at not being able to throw a society wedding for their sometimes wayward daughter. The Donovans' Catholicism was just another obstacle to be overcome. The Duke was always persuasive and his visceral attraction to Betty was never in doubt. They were always a physical couple and, for the Duke, this probably felt like love. As for me, I never noticed any obvious animosity between the Duke and the Donovans, so I guess he somehow won them over, a result he would have considered inevitable.

Having completed basic training with a new wife and a child on the way, the Duke was assigned to the 513th Military Intelligence Brigade in Ft. Monmouth, New Jersey. Bobby was born there, and I joined the family a little less than a year later, just as things were heating up in the Persian Gulf. I've never known any details, most of which remain classified, even now, but the Duke was intimately involved in planning and implementing intelligence operations in both Desert Shield and Desert Storm. He was deployed to Southwest Asia in early 1990 and didn't return until May 1991. He was honorably discharged as a first lieutenant, but his service never left him. Like many others, it marked him both literally and emotionally. Possessed of a Purple Heart, a Bronze Star, a jagged six-inch scar on the outside of his left forearm, and an arresting streak of white hair above his left temple, the Duke rarely spoke of any of it and my mother learned to stop asking. I learned eventually that he spent a lot of time alone in the desert meeting operatives and agents. I know he was involved in abducting and interrogating Baath Party officials, and I know he sharpened the beliefs about human motivation he transferred as best he could to his professional and family lives, for better or worse. The Duke, having faced and administered death himself, knew how precarious his grip on the planet actually was. He came to believe that human interaction derived from a single premise: I want your stuff. How much am I willing to cooperate before resorting to naked force to get it?

Thinking of this brought me back to the morning in May 2009 when I returned home to the condo in downtown Gainesville I shared with my brother. I had spent the night at the house near campus where my girlfriend lived with two friends. Bobby and I were roommates, but we were also teammates on the UF track team. In fact, we had just competed in the SEC outdoor championships held in Gainesville that year and were looking forward to the regional qualifying meet the following week and the NCAA championship meet two weeks after that. As a competitor in the decathlon, a series of ten events reflecting broad athletic skills, I was pretty good at many things but great at none. Bobby, on the other hand, was a stone-cold killer in the 400-meter run, the most brutal race of all as I knew too well from having to run it as part of the decathlon. Watch the end of a competitive 400-meter race and you will see athletes reaching deep within themselves to summon strength not provided by physical training alone. Where that strength comes from—if it comes—varies from person to person, but in Bobby's case I knew it came from his unslaked need for his father's approval. For as long as I could remember, Bobby viewed everything he did as a reflection on the Duke, who was always watching, however impassively.

It's funny how these things go in families, but Bobby was clearly our mother's favorite all along, with his gifts as an artist, his amiable personality, and ready smile. He never quite reached six feet in height, but he was wiry, very strong, and built to run. And he looked a lot like the Duke, dark and ramrod straight. I, on the other hand, passed my brother and father in height during tenth grade and topped out at six feet four inches. Blond with blue eyes, intellectually curious but not particularly focused, I clearly favored the Donovans, but somehow always seemed to find the Duke's favor as Bobby and I grew up. Transgressions for which Bobby faced strict punishment never drew even a raised voice when committed by me. Who knows? Maybe the Duke had lower expectations for his second son. Looking back at it now, that was probably it.

None of this came between Bobby and me. We could not have been closer had we been born twins. I actually begged my parents to let me skip third grade so I could be in Bobby's class, which they allowed. After that, even though our interests and activities were very different, we were best friends as well as brothers, which is to say that I was not ready to find my brother's cold, dead body when I opened the front door that Saturday morning. At first I thought he was sleeping, stretched out on the couch wearing his blue running shorts and white "Florida Track" tank top.

"Wake up, Robert, a new day awaits!"

There was no sound or movement and then, in the fraction of a second before adrenaline supercharges all senses, there was the smell. Watching the discovery of a body on TV or in a movie doesn't prepare you for the reality of it. Upon death, all muscles relax, including sphincter muscles. The resulting stench slapped me into the realization that something was very wrong. Covering the ten feet to the couch in two strides, I instinctively reached down to touch Bobby's face. It was cool. I stupidly shook his shoulders, knowing already he was dead but unable to stop myself from a pointless search for life. I checked for a pulse in his throat before stepping back and allowing this new reality to enter my conscious mind. I found myself staring at the peaceful expression on his face and the hands clasped calmly on his chest, partially covering a plain white envelope.

Without thinking, I leaned in and slipped the envelope out from under his fingers. It was unmarked and unsealed. I reflexively opened it and found a tri-folded page of the creamy yellow stationery Bobby used to thoughtfully write thank-you or congratulatory notes to his friends and family members in response to gifts or achievements. Unfolding the page, I found Bobby's testament; beautifully written in his looping, exquisite calligraphy, rendered in the dark blue ink he favored for use with his prized Mont Blanc fountain pen. As my throat tightened, I began to read and, within seconds, knew what had happened and why. I knew the first call had to go to 911 in the event my cell phone records were ever reviewed, but the second call had to go to the Duke. And, as always, he answered immediately.

"Duke Girard speaking."

"Dad, it's Jack. Bobby's dead. He's gone."

"Jack, hold on a second and take a breath. Where are you?"

"In the condo. In the living room. He's on the couch. He killed himself. Oh my God, he did it!"

"Jack, please, how do you know he killed himself. Is there a gun? Did he hang himself?" The Duke always cut to the chase.

"No, no. He's lying on the couch like he's asleep. But there's a note."

The Duke's mind was racing ahead.

"A note? Where's the note?"

"In my hand. It was on his chest and I picked it up. It was in an envelope and . . . and . . . I read it."

"So you have the note and there is no other indication that it was a suicide?"

"Well, no, not that I can tell. I mean, I don't see a pill bottle or anything."

"Okay. Jack, listen to me," he said with his well-practiced voice of command. "Have you called 911?"

"Yes."

"Good. They'll be there very soon. Take the note and the envelope into your room and put them between your mattress and the box spring. Go into Bobby's bathroom and see if there are any pill bottles on the counter or in his medicine cabinet. I'm sure there will be, but if there aren't, call me back. Don't touch the bottles! Leave them where they are. Then go back to the living room and wait. When the paramedics get there, tell them this is exactly what you found when you walked in. You called it in right away and were waiting ever since. You say the same thing to the police. They will do a search, but it will focus on Bobby, and they'll find the pills. If they ask about a note—and they might not—you repeat that you just found him on the couch and called 911. Do you have this, Jack? We need to get off the phone."

"Why, Dad? Why am I hiding the note?"

"Son, Robert Kennedy Girard did not commit suicide. We will not give in on that conclusion until the ME says otherwise and maybe not even then. My son does not deserve that stain on his memory. You get me? Am I clear on this?"

"Yes, sir."

"Then go on and do your duty to your brother."

Which I did. Unflinchingly. And it went pretty much as the Duke described. Eventually, the medical examiner concluded that Bobby died accidentally by taking pain medication earlier prescribed to help him with persistent tendonitis in his surgically repaired right knee coupled with alcohol, presumably ingested during that fateful Friday evening.

Which was true as far as it went. Bobby and I had been out to a happy hour in a downtown bar with our track teammates before I went on a date and he went home to escape the trap he evidently found himself in. A haunting memory—has it changed over the years of reliving it?—is of the last bro-hug we exchanged as I was getting ready to leave. He looked up, slightly unfocused, and said, "The future is all yours, baby brother. Don't fuck it up."

To which I responded—my last words: "Don't drive home." I gave him a mock punch in the gut as I turned for the door, chuckling as I went.

How do some memories persist with such apparent clarity while others fade and still others metamorphose into something slightly new with each reflection? Do I actually see the expression on my brother's face as I walk away, had I only turned to look? I think repetition is at the root of it, judging by my own experience.

CHAPTER SIX

Feeling only slightly less foggy as I arrived on the mainland, I elected to turn off bustling U.S. 1 at 152nd Street and travel east and north on historic Old Cutler Road. The meandering two-lane road was originally cut through hardwood hammocks in the 1880s to connect the coastal farming town of Cutler with the village of Coconut Grove. Following a natural limestone ridge running along the edge of Biscayne Bay, it eventually became an obvious high-elevation choice for the construction of mansions on multi-acre estates cascading down to the clear blue water. One such mansion was built in the 1920s just north of what is now Arvida Parkway by August Joyce Donovan, a real estate investor from New York who had the good sense to diversify his investments to include stakes in several trading and shipping companies, capitalizing on the burgeoning commerce between the United States, Cuba, and other Caribbean nations. It was rum that ultimately made Donovan rich enough to shrug off the Depression like a persistent fly at a picnic.

As I approached the old Donovan house from the southwest through the magnificent tree tunnel formed by majestic live oak, banyan, and gumbo limbo trees lining the road, I was struck by the shimmering, ethereal quality of the light filtering through the branches from the sun setting over my left shoulder. I never thought of myself as a sentimental person, or even a particularly spiritual one, but I was possessed of an image of my mother's and brother's arched arms above me, linking hands eternally like these seemingly ageless works of nature reaching across the man-made road. For the first time since my phone rang hours earlier, I smiled.

I was snapped from this momentary peace by sight of the impervious gray limestone walls bordering the Donovans' property emerging on my right. I slowed to peer through the old iron gate at the imposing main house built from the same stone set back from the road and shrouded by carefully tended and pruned Royal Poinciana trees. Farther north I passed the second gate fronting the crushed shell driveway leading back to the house but also revealing a two-story garage building, the second floor of which contained the two-room apartment that had served as my home after my graduation from law school in 2012 until my flight to Key West in 2016.

My mother had long since broken with her parents and much of her extended family, primarily by rejecting the Catholicism that played such a large role in their lives. The Duke, a lapsed-Protestant atheist, encouraged this, although he believed each side was irrationally unforgiving of the superstitions of the other. For Betty, the fundamental dogma of papal infallibility on issues of morality and faith was finally unacceptable. She sincerely believed there could be no intermediary in her ultimate spiritual life. She could be educated, advised, and counseled, but, in the end, morality and faith were hers alone to assess. Obedience was never her strong suit, as she demonstrated again and again.

Despite all of this, she prevailed upon her parents to let me live rent-free in the garage apartment on their property while I studied for the bar exam and got started in my legal career. My grandparents were sensitive to the pain my mother continued to cope with since Bobby's death, some of it inflicted by them, and believed, I think, that this gesture of generosity could serve as a bridge to family unity. Knowing my mother and the resentments she suppressed in different ways, I knew that was never going to happen, but I was nonetheless happy for the free apartment. And it gave me a chance to develop adult relationships with my grandparents, who really only knew me as one of the two boys splashing in their pool during the occasional but stressful family get-togethers. Much had changed since then.

For me, the days, months, and years since Bobby died were consumed by serious, mind-numbing effort. I had graduated with Bobby and then immediately started law school after his death, making my way onto the Law Review and participating in as many activities as could be packed into a twenty-four-hour day. Sleep became something of a stranger and not something I missed. When I did sleep, my dreams consistently centered on the loss of a loved thing, often a dog, often involving a panicked search through a forest at night in a driving rainstorm. I would wake up soaked in sweat, heart racing but certain, at least, that I'd never owned a dog. I spent no time analyzing the obvious symbolism and ignored the idea that I was somehow wounded. I was a Girard, after all. We persevered. We moved forward, one labored step at a time. As the Duke would often remind us, "Even God can't change the past." So I spent three years living moment by moment, each day knowing that when it ended another day would come, providing incremental distance between me and my brother's personal day of reckoning.

At the end of it, I had a law degree, a resume stuffed with achievement, and offers to work at prestigious law firms across the state. I turned down all of them and chose to start my career at Duke Girard & Associates, unable to resist the inexorable pull of the Duke's gravity. At a certain level, it made perfect sense: I would receive excellent training on the nuts and bolts of developing cases for trial and the tricks of presenting them to jurors. But there would be no partnership as a reward for my hard work. The firm's name was not Duke Girard & Partners, after all. Looking back, I think I was attracted to the short horizon the Duke was offering. Somehow, I knew instinctively I was in no condition to make big decisions about my long-term future. And then, before I knew it, those decisions were made for me.

CHAPTER SEVEN

By now I had left Old Cutler at the Coco Plum Circle and continued north along similarly scenic Ingraham Highway, Douglas Road, and then Main Highway, which led into the village center of Coconut Grove, annexed by the city of Miami in 1925 but still charmed by vestiges of its history as the oldest continuous settlement in Miami-Dade County. Turning down the slope of the coral ridge leading to Biscayne Bay on McFarlane Road, I was struck as always by the physical beauty of the waterfront parks and the bay itself, dotted with sailboats of all sizes at their moorings and glistening reflections of the fading afternoon sun. My family of four had spent many hours and days together on that bay, fishing, diving, and boating, and I was now very near my meeting with the Duke, the last of us other than me. As I eased along South Bayshore Drive, the last dull ache in my head was displaced by a jolt of anxiety and anger as I considered the reasons I had not traveled this path in more than two years.

Things had started well enough for me as a junior associate in my father's firm. There were twelve lawyers in all at the time, but none of them had less than five years of experience. The Duke liked to hire well-trained lawyers from large defense firms who had demonstrated talent in the courtroom but chafed against the rigid structures those firms imposed. If they were sufficiently aggressive, self-confident, and charismatic, they could easily double their already generous incomes by trading their stuffy but well-reputed associations for the fast, hold-on-to-your-hat professional life offered by Duke Girard & Associates. Advertising and the Duke's reputation brought the cases in the door and, ultimately, the Duke decided how they were distributed, usually keeping the highest profile and most lucrative cases for himself. After that it was up to the individual lawyers to obtain the highest collectable settlements and judgments as efficiently as possible, utilizing the team of paralegals and legal assistants to carry much of the load.

As a junior associate, I handled low-level legal work that couldn't be done by the paralegals and was too time-intensive to be performed efficiently by the fee-chasing senior lawyers. This mostly involved researching and writing briefs on the more challenging legal and evidentiary issues that arose and tracking down and speaking to witnesses. When I did get my chances to argue motions before judges or examine witnesses in the trials of cases I assisted on, it became clear, to me at least, that I had some aptitude for the work.

In one case, the Duke let me cross-examine a pharmaceutical manufacturing executive about the timing of a company investigation into reported side effects of the drug that was the subject of the trial. The executive had testified in his deposition that he was unaware of issues with the drug until shortly before he ordered the investigation. After the deposition, we uncovered emails copied to the executive discussing complaints to the company's consumer hotline by patients describing the side effects six months earlier. At trial, the executive simply testified that he was aware of "sporadic" reports from consumers in the preceding months, but ordered the investigation after receiving multiple reports from doctors relating to the problem. The company's lawyer should have handled the discrepancy in testimony in his direct examination, but didn't. I think the Duke wanted to see if I noticed it and, if so, how I would handle it. To me, it seemed pretty obvious at the time, but impeaching witnesses with prior testimony is apparently a struggle for a lot of lawyers. It requires a command of all of the relevant testimony in the case. It went like this:

ME: Mr. Jenkins, you testified earlier this morning that you were aware that consumers—the people actually taking your drug—were calling the company hotline to complain about side effects—the very same side effects at issue in this case— six months before the investigation started, correct?

WITNESS: Yes, that's true.

ME: Mr. Jenkins, do you recall being deposed in this case on January 23, 2014?

WITNESS: Yes.

ME: At that time, you swore to tell the truth, just like you did here today, right?

WITNESS: Yes, I did.

ME: And you understood at the time that the consequences for lying under oath were exactly the same as they are today in this courtroom, correct?

WITNESS: Yes.

ME: Well, then, I'm puzzled, Mr. Jenkins, because in your deposition at page 143, line 12, the following question and answer occurs: Question: Were you aware of issues with or complaints about the drug prior to the doctors' reports you relied on to initiate the investigation? Answer: No. Mr. Jenkins, you gave that answer to that question at that time, right?

WITNESS: Yes, but—

ME: "Yes" will do, Mr. Jenkins. You gave that answer at that time because you were trying to hide the fact that the company was aware of problem side effects of the drug a full six months before you saw fit to investigate, six months during which many others—including our client—were afflicted with those effects, isn't that right?

WITNESS: Well, no, it just seemed that the problem was insignificant at the time and I forgot about it when I was deposed.

ME: The problem was "insignificant"? You said, "Insignificant"? Thank you, Mr. Jenkins. I have no further questions.

As you might imagine, the Duke made a masterful closing argument and we won the case, recovering a lot of money for our client. Afterward, some members of the jury said that the executive's apparent indifference to complaints by ordinary people was a deciding factor in their decision to award punitive damages. The Duke was apparently impressed by my ability to seize upon the issue and squeeze it on the spur of the moment. So, when he decided to take on civil rights and discrimination cases as a way to further ingratiate himself with his target audiences, he put me in charge of the new cases, to be conducted under his supervision. These cases, brought under state and federal statutes, were comparatively low-dollar because of statutory limits on recoverable damages. So it made sense to have the lowest-paid lawyer handle them once I had established a baseline of competence.

Nonetheless, one interesting element of the authorizing statutes was that they permitted an award of attorney's fees to the winner. As a practical matter, this only came into play when a case actually went to trial; if it settled, it was subject to a percentage contingent fee like the other kinds of cases handled by the firm. But when a case went to trial and we won, we were entitled to submit a petition for an award of attorney's fees. The presiding judge made the final award based on several factors, but the starting point of the analysis was the number of hours spent by the lawyers on all of the tasks associated with the case. Keeping meticulous track of the work performed was the responsibility of the submitting lawyers, thus creating a challenge for a firm like ours where attorneys were not ordinarily required to keep track of their time, focusing instead on the dollars brought through the door pursuant to contingent fee contracts in each case.

The Duke had already decided that the publicity of the civil rights cases we sought would more than pay for the cost of handling them by way of referrals of medical malpractice and product liability cases. But that didn't mean he wouldn't maximize any chance to squeeze income from a winner. With the help of his legal assistant, the Duke devised a system of time entry for civil rights cases that essentially involved me submitting an email to the assistant on a daily basis setting out what I had done on each case along with the number of hours, broken down to the nearest tenth of an hour. He would likewise submit his time and the assistant maintained a rolling spread-sheet for each case reflecting all of the entries. This was fine as far as it went.

It's easy now in hindsight to see how easily manipulated these entries were. Even though I had real experience with the Duke massaging reality to suit his immediate needs, I never thought for a second he would jeopardize his lucrative law practice for a few thousand dollars here or there. I soon realized he wasn't willing to risk his own practice but was more than willing to sacrifice mine when an attorney at a defense firm coincidentally handling two of our fee petitions at the same time noticed that I had nine-hour time entries in both cases on the same day, which is physically impossible. Upon being notified of this, the Duke expressed appropriate shock and dismay, assuring the judge and opposing counsel that he would investigate the matter and take action, including self-reporting to the Florida Bar, which grants and revokes law licenses in the state. It's hard to believe now, but I was unaware of most of this until the deal was done, at the conclusion of the Duke's "confidential" investigation. The upshot was that the firm took no fee on the two cases and the sole culprit revealed by the investigation—me—would receive a six-month suspension of the right to practice.

The Duke appealed to my innate loyalty when he told me what was arranged: "Jack, you've always been a great team player. Your whole life you've been willing to sacrifice your personal glory to benefit the team, even when it cost you. Of course, I remember your senior year of high school when you agreed to play quarter-back on the football team rather than your natural receiver position because there was nobody better that year. You were good at quarterback but not nearly as good as you would have been play-ing wideout. I know that cost you scholarship offers, but you never complained. You took it like the man I raised you to be because you valued team success over individual achievement. I never forgot that and I was proud of you. Today I'm asking you to make another sacrifice."

He then explained his scheme to make more money on the discrimination cases by adding time in the system to the submissions I was making to his assistant on a daily basis. He had too much at stake to risk padding his own time. But he believed that in the highly unlikely event the scheme was discovered, a junior lawyer like me could withstand a slap on the wrist without real damage to his career. He considered it an almost comical turn of events that two cases filed two years apart not only wouldn't settle but would then end up being tried back-to-back before the same judge and opposed by the same law firm. That was the only way the post-trial fee process could have given that defense lawyer the opportunity to compare the bills. The Duke wrapped up his presentation with a sweetener.

"Think of it this way, Jack. You're getting a paid vacation for six months. Go to Europe, go on safari. Take the time to do things you haven't even dreamed of these last seven years. I can't pretend to know how painful these years have been for you. For me, the knife slides deeper into my heart when I see you as I'm seeing you now—emotionless, deadpan, your face expressing nothing. I can't help but remember how much time you and your brother spent laughing. It's the way I think of you. I want to see you that way again. Please take this time to find yourself, Jack."

He paused for a moment before reaching forward and handing me what appeared to be a check.

"And I'm very aware of your hard work and exemplary service to this firm. Which is why I've decided to give you this bonus of $200,000."

I was stunned. We were seated in his glass-walled penthouse office overlooking the bay in downtown Miami, separated by his massive glass and onyx desk. He made no move to touch me but watched me intently as I swallowed and digested this extraordinary fait accompli: the check lay on the edge of the desk before me, a final punctuation mark in the Duke's carefully drafted script. I knew in an instant it was hopeless. To contest this or proclaim innocence was career suicide. The Duke and his well-paid assistant controlled the documents. The Duke himself controlled both sides of the narrative. Not only would he implicate me, he would also poison the minds of the friends and professional cronies who would decide my fate. Many owed favors to the Duke; no one owed me anything.

I took the check. Looking back, I have mixed feelings about rolling over as I did, but that money became Jack's Hideaway and allowed me to carve out the beginning of a life that was mine alone. I eventually got my law license back and started handling cases here and there for friends and acquaintances I met through the bar. Mostly, these were landlord/tenant disputes or insurance claims of one kind or another. Although I couldn't have made a living this way, it felt good to help people out of jams that might seem unimportant to others but meant everything to them. Fortunately, the bar was making money and I could afford this decidedly nonprofit approach to my legal career. Positive word-of-mouth from clients was also good for the bar, a benefit I hadn't thought of when I started.

But I didn't know this path to the future existed when I silently snatched the check off the desk and turned for the door. The Duke's assistant, bespectacled and primly dressed, lingered just outside. She began to speak, but I silenced her with a glance. My stature and the fury radiating from me like heat from a lava flow kept the staff and the other staring lawyers at bay as I reached the elevator and exited the Duke's fiefdom for what turned out to be the last time.

CHAPTER EIGHT

I was almost there. I turned east onto Rockerman Road as I had so many times before over the last two decades. Notorious as a drug drop during the 1980s because it fronted a short canal opening directly on Biscayne Bay and the Atlantic Ocean beyond, Rockerman always maintained a place in Miami lore. My father bought one of the fourteen canal-side houses in 1999 when Bobby was eleven and I was ten. This was the first sign of the Duke's success after racing through law school at the University of Miami upon his return from the war and then starting his own firm after a brief stint as an assistant state prosecutor. The comfortable four-bedroom, three-bath ranch-style house was a little run-down and needed upgrading, but it had a hundred-foot seawall and a boatlift for vessels up to thirty feet. Because Coconut Grove had been supplanted by Miami Beach as the hip place to be, the price seemed reasonable, and the Duke always bought low. Bobby and I spent our best years there, at least the way I thought about it. I can't say now that Bobby would agree.

As I came to the familiar address, I encountered the monstrous modernist structure I had heard about but never seen. In the years I had been away, the Duke had torn down our comfortable, memory-filled home and replaced it with this six-bedroom, seven-bath glass-faced edifice covering virtually the entire lot with no thought to concepts like perspective and scale. According to my mother in our relatively sparse communication, the Duke had used Bobby's death to justify the project, claiming she had not been able to move past the tragedy because she was confronted by endless images of her lost son every day as she moved from room to room.

But she knew as well as I did that the Duke's real purpose was to destroy the reminder of all that had been lost and replace it with a monument to all he had gained. Both of his sons were absent from his life and his wife had retreated to the comfort of her own thoughts, aided by vodka and Valium. She had begun to spend her days on the flagstone terrace behind the old house, staring across the canal into the greenery of Kennedy Park and beyond. She had little to say, to the Duke or anyone else. Whatever her thoughts were, she wasn't sharing and, at the time, I wasn't thinking about any role I might have played in her despair. For the Duke, Betty's maudlin sentimentality was unacceptable. The future waited for no one, so he bought the Miami Beach condominium to serve as a temporary living space and brought the wrecking ball to Rockerman Road. When the new house was finally complete, just six months ago, the Duke came to understand the full price he had paid.

Now I stood at the massive mahogany double doors that neither my mother nor I had ever stepped through. For when the Duke had announced it was time to move in, Betty responded by saying she was staying in the condo. She followed up by personally serving him with a divorce petition. According to my mother, the Duke barely blinked and acted like he knew it was coming, which he probably did.

Nothing big in the Miami legal community escaped his notice, and this qualified as big. I never knew all the details because I was high-mindedly toiling away in law school as my parents faced the loss of their first son, but my mother never accepted the Duke's revision of Bobby's death. She was a truth-teller, believing that nothing good came from suppression. And she knew the whole truth. I don't know what passed between them in those earliest days and weeks, what pact was reached. But I do know that Betty elected to keep the secret, as I did. For her, the personal cost was high. Her natural exuberance became muted and she withdrew from interactions with family and friends who were offering comfort in support of a false narrative. Valium provided a substitute leveling of ragged emotions, and vodka provided a daily escape into painless oblivion.

And then somehow, and for some reason, my mother emerged from her self-imposed purgatory during her last year on earth, the divorce petition serving as a gateway to more than just personal freedom. Something about her life across the causeway in Miami Beach roused her, leading to divorce, it's true, but also inspiring her to begin painting again, which, for her, was life-affirming. She depicted water scenes with sailboats, masts bending and sails billowing with promise, as she remembered from her childhood on the bay. Something had triggered a return to living. I didn't know then what it was.

CHAPTER NINE

I knocked on the door. I hoped to see our longtime housekeeper, Marta, the patient teacher of Spanish to Bobby and me as we grew up, pull open the door and serve as a much-needed intermediary in my first encounter with the Duke. It wasn't to be. I heard the crisp staccato rhythm of the Duke's Ferragamo loafers crossing the marble floor, then a pause. The door swung open and my father, starting with my flip-flops, faded board shorts, and well-worn blue Gators tee shirt, appraised me, finally settling his black eyes on my unshaved face and windblown hair. "You look like you could use a drink, Jack."

I responded, "Truer words were never spoken."

And there was Marta, carrying a silver tray, bearing twin martini glasses filled with what I knew were Maker's Mark Manhattans, expertly crafted with only the slightest hint of vermouth. I took one and swallowed half without waiting for the toast I knew the Duke wanted to offer. He had probably been rehearsing it. His moment stolen, the Duke seized his glass and turned to walk back through the cavernous entrance hall toward an open doorway on the left. Always immaculate, he wore uncreased flax-colored linen trousers with a perfectly tailored black print raw silk shirt. His black hair, professionally tousled, betrayed the first few gray strands of aging, further accentuating the white streak he brought back from Iraq. Marta smiled at me; I knew she had my back. I leaned down to kiss her on the cheek before following my father into what turned out to be his library, windowless and dark, filled floor to ten-foot ceiling along the walls with shelves packed with books he collected over the years, including many valuable first editions of literary and philosophical works. The polished teakwood floor was partially covered by a brilliantly complex Persian rug, upon which rested two massive dark leather club chairs. The wall behind was dominated by an original Vinikoff oil painting of an Everglades scene, rich in shades and shadows missed by less accomplished artists. The Duke turned and beckoned me to sit. A bottle of Old Rip Van Winkle ten-year-old bourbon and two rocks glasses sat on the side table between the two chairs. The Duke meant business.

Sitting down, he said, "Jack, let's get right to it. I know you had a deep connection to your mother, even though you barely saw her these last few years."

He paused to see if I would react to this initial shot across the bow. I didn't. He never did quite capture, in his own rigid thinking, the layers and subtleties of my relationship with my mother. I never thought of it as deep, but it covered a lot of ground.

I eased into the opposite chair and swallowed what remained of my drink. The eight-hour fog in my brain was lifting. With a nod, I encouraged the Duke to continue as I set my empty glass on the table.

"There's going to be a service at Plymouth Congregational on Tuesday, but I don't expect a big turnout. The Donovans have already said they're not coming. Which means none of their friends are coming."

He hesitated. I knew he was considering delivering a rant about the Donovans' rigid Catholic attitude toward suicide, which had first loomed over us when Bobby's cause of death was still in limbo. He sipped his drink and stayed on point.

"I know they're devastated and will deal with this in their own way. No parents should outlive their children, as I know too well. The point is, if you plan to see your grandparents, you'll have to go to them."

Again, I said nothing and waited. Of course, as an experienced trial lawyer, the Duke knew this tactic for drawing out a witness possessed of information he isn't sure he wants to divulge. Silence is often irresistible, as I learned myself during the four cases I had tried and won during my short time at the firm. So the Duke set his martini glass down and busied himself opening the bottle of bourbon and pouring two fingers each into the rocks glasses between us. Picking up the one nearest to me, I savored the smoky bourbon and contemplated what should come next. I elected to speak, ceding the Duke a victory of sorts. As I sipped, I said, "Obviously, there's a reason you got me here today instead of Tuesday. I'm sure it's not for consolation, either giving or receiving. Why are we here?"

I asked this question for the second time that day and was just as curious about the answer.

The Duke eyed me with a combination of irritation and respect, having long forgotten the rhetorical sparring we once did when our relationship was less strained. Or, more accurately, when our relationship existed. From the time I began reading and developing thoughts of my own, we argued about everything; from the wisdom of the Dolphins' draft strategy to the accuracy of the fundamental principle espoused by the Duke's philosophical hero, Friedrich Nietzsche: the single defining characteristic of the human animal is the will to power. As a teen with a bit of Christian religious training thanks to my mother's casual feel-good ethos, this dark thought was as aggravating as it was difficult to dispel, particularly in an argument, however civil, with the Duke and his patina of hard-earned experiential credibility. I could never match that with mere words.

"Son," he would say, "it's only when you exist in an environment free from the norms and constraints of civil society that you learn your true nature, whatever it might be. You haven't learned this yet. Maybe you never will."

How do you respond to that at age fourteen?

Bobby stayed clear of these battles, accepting the Duke's wisdom like Moses receiving the commandments. He never noticed the Duke's disappointment in this, but Bobby wasn't one for intellectual wordplay. He liked a clear path and a clearer conscience. Intolerant of confusion, Bobby opted for certainty every time.

Swirling his bourbon to arouse a more robust scent, the Duke moved the conversation closer to his purpose.

"Okay, Jack. Tell me if the name Julio Guzman means anything to you."

"Sure, he's a Colombian rich guy who owns a healthcare network or something like that. I think you've sued him before, right? What does he have to do with anything?"

"I don't know if he does. That's the problem. Everything about this spells suicide, and the police are moving directly to that conclusion. There was a note, an open pill bottle, and no evidence of forced entry or foul play. I'm just having a hard time accepting that Betty killed herself. Until Bobby died, the worst thing that ever happened to her was not getting into Harvard. But Bobby's death knocked her down hard. You weren't around for much of it, but every bit of life left her then—except she kept right on breathing, waking up every day, and then rolling one day into another. Sedated as she was, never once did she consider taking her own life. Maybe there was some Catholic left in her, or maybe just being alive was good enough. But I never worried about suicide. Maybe an accident? Of course. But never suicide."

He paused there and took a long swallow, staring off into the dim recesses of the room.

I interjected: "Julio Guzman? How does he fit?"

The Duke turned to look at me, his eyes simmering with barely controlled anger.

"Your mother was having an affair with him. I don't know exactly when it started."

The Duke ran his fingers through his hair as he considered how to verbalize what he was feeling, or at least as much of what he was feeling as he was willing to share.

"It may seem hard to believe, but I didn't know anything about it until after your mother hit me with the divorce petition. I was spending most of my time on this side of the causeway, what with work and the construction of the new house and every other damn thing. Lots of nights at the Four Seasons on Brickell while she was over there doing . . . whatever she was doing."

Those words hung in the air for a moment. This was a surprise to me but not a shock. Something had lifted my mother from the abyss; maybe this was it.

"He lives in the penthouse of our building. I guess I knew he was there, but I never paid him any attention, which was probably a mistake. He's divorced, good looking, wealthy, sort of a smooth operator, judging by the stories in the *Herald* and on social media. Just the sort of guy who would notice a woman like your mother—beautiful but a little worn down."

I reacted.

"Screw him, Dad! Maybe you should have paid a little more attention to your wife!"

"Very easy words to say, Jack. Very easy. But you don't know what the fuck you're talking about because you weren't here! Do you remember how your mother was living when you started at the firm? I don't seem to remember you spending much time with her. Oh, I know, you had your own problems and a career to get started. Living with the Donovans was a helluva lot easier than living here. But it was your mother who made that happen because she didn't want to drag you down. You paid that back by running away to Key West. So don't you lecture me, boy!"

That was a gut punch. I never thought of the garage apartment on Old Cutler as altruism by anyone but my grandparents. But I could see Betty deciding she wasn't strong enough to fix herself but was capable of pushing her son away from the convent of misery she inhabited then. I felt tears welling up, which I could not let the Duke have the satisfaction of seeing.

"So why are we talking about this?"

He fixed me again with his best courtroom stare.

"Okay, Jack. I'll get there. But let me give you a little more information. I had one of the investigators, your old buddy Steve Amos, do a little digging."

Steve was a retired FBI agent with a variety of skills that were useful to the law firm and its owner.

"It turns out that Guzman has some partners in the health-care business. Two of those partners are boyhood friends of his who continue to operate their primary business, which, ironically enough, puts thousands of Floridians into the healthcare system every year. Yes, Jack, they're cocaine wholesalers who now profit at both ends. But the really interesting thing is that Steve's friends at the DEA believe Guzman was and still is a partner in the drug business. They were always looking for ways to launder money, and hospitals and clinics were perfect for it. Expensive equipment, supplies, and consultants are routinely ordered, and no one notices if some of them never materialize out of the morass of red tape. No one cares if uninsured procedures are performed only on paper as long as they're paid for. They picked Guzman to head up the operation because he had never been arrested and had an MBA from Wharton." He paused. "The problem is that all of this is conjectural. No one yet has tried to prove any of it. But as Nietzsche points out, 'There are no facts; only interpretations.' I'm pretty satisfied with the interpretation I'm giving you."

Just as I was about to ask a couple of obvious questions, Marta poked her head through the door to announce that dinner was on the table. In the Girard household, that marked the end of all talk of business and the beginning of an hour-long period of appreciation for what we had, both individually and as a family. We would talk about the food, sports, books, art, politics, relationships, music, even religion. Anything other than money or the various ways of accumulating it. It was a Donovan tradition that even the Duke came to appreciate. I recalled my brother attempting to imitate the impenetrable Southern drawl of our peewee football coach and my parents bursting out with unrestrained laughter at the innocence of it. Now, as I rose, it was painful to remember how seemingly happy we were for so many years together. But were we really? Or were we all just acting our parts in a series of one-act plays? My perspective certainly changed, but those pleasant family dinners actually happened. I'm pretty sure they did.

CHAPTER TEN

After a somber repast of Marta's empanadas and my childhood favorite, boliche, a Cuban pot roast stuffed with ham and simmered in water with onions until deliciously soft, the Duke and I walked through the vast and starkly appointed house to the newly installed pool deck, where carefully tended tropical landscaping surrounded an irregularly shaped limestone pool and a tiki hut, complete with wet bar, ice machine, and four bamboo and leather stools. Marta had thoughtfully transferred the bottle of Old Rip Van Winkle from the library to the bar, along with fresh glasses. I hadn't said much at dinner; picking at my food, as I wondered if the Duke thought at all about the two Girards missing from the table. Probably not, judging by his appetite.

Now, he took a seat at the bar and poured more bourbon into two glasses. I sat down and peered past the pool in the enveloping darkness to the dock where the Duke's new 44-foot Contender center console fishing boat, complete with tuna tower, radar dome, and a triple configuration of Yamaha 425cc engines, nuzzled against its padded mooring. Dock lights, along with the twinkling landscape lighting amid the foliage, cast the boat's navy-blue hull in an ominous profile. That boat was a fish-killer. Then, to my surprise, I saw the comparatively proletarian 26-foot Intrepid center console of my youth, raised out of the water on a boatlift behind the Contender. In the dim light it looked exactly as it had when I was twelve, although I could see that the original engines had been replaced. Breaking into the silence I asked, "So why did you hold onto *Betty's Boys* when you bought the Contender?"

The Duke looked over at the boat and appeared to consider his response.

"I meant to trade it in. I even had it at the marina when I was taking possession of the new one. But looking at it there at the dock, I saw every nick and scratch on the hull as a reminder of all the adventures you, me, Betty, and Bobby had through the years. I suppose more Bobby and me. Anyway, I decided then and there to keep it. And I upgraded it a little. Plus, it's a little easier to handle when I'm out by myself. Maybe I'm just sentimental."

I stifled a snort of laughter by taking a long swallow of bourbon. The Duke was anything but sentimental, as I thought of him then. There had to be a utilitarian reason for him to have kept the boat, and maybe it was as simple as ease of operation. But I knew that Contender pretty much operated itself. There was something else, and I figured bringing up Bobby offered a clue.

It's true that all of us spent a lot of time on the water, situated as we were a mere hundred yards from Biscayne Bay. But as Bobby and I reached our teen years, our interests diverged a little. I was drawn to team sports like football and basketball that demanded a lot of practice and training time on land. I still loved wake-boarding and spear-fishing on the weekends, but Bobby was different. He was a waterman from the start. There was nothing you could do in the water or on a boat that he didn't attack with gusto. Underwater he swam like an eel and had the lungs of a dolphin, which certainly helped him on the running track.

But for Bobby, the best part of his attraction to the water was the time alone it gave him with our father, whom Bobby idolized. After all of his experiences in the desert during the Gulf War, the Duke also found comfort in the vast ocean and was glad to explore all it could offer with his first son. I never felt any jealousy about their relationship, and they always welcomed me aboard when I wanted to come along. But those two could handle lines, back down on a big fish, or spot schooling mahi without uttering a word. They each found a singular peace on the water I admired but didn't fully understand—then.

I could easily have allowed the conversation to meander among our shared memories of my brother, and a part of me would have welcomed this exploration of recollections too painful to cognize for many years, but I knew I had to confront the Duke's pre-dinner revelations. The man himself was now as still as a July night on the bay. His eyes were fixed on the Intrepid, his expression betraying no emotion. The Duke's feelings were so deeply buried and enshrouded by hard experience that no bourbon-fueled reminiscence would uncover them anyway, so I circled back to Julio Guzman.

"Okay, Dad, I want to move back to what we were talking about before dinner. You've said that my mother was having an affair with Guzman and that Guzman is still a partner in a cocaine operation that launders money through his hospital network. How does either one of those things figure in Betty's death?"

"Well, Jack, neither does, by itself. But what if you add in the fact that Guzman had broken it off with Betty? That Betty was taking things too seriously for him? That her filing for a divorce was the last thing in the world he wanted because it revealed her expectations for their shared future? Her expectations did not match his, Jack. He liked things the way they were,"

I was skeptical of this as a motive for murder.

"So he somehow managed to fake her suicide to . . . what? Put a final end to their relationship? That's a little extreme."

The Duke was nodding. "Yes, I agree. I can see exactly how Guzman looked at it. This would be an aggravation, but nothing he hadn't dealt with before when it came to women. What would be different about Betty? This is where the real speculation comes in. The rest of it I'm certain is true."

He resisted as he waited for me to glance his way, then fixed me with the look meant to convince reluctant jurors to embrace his vision of a case.

"Betty knew the truth about him, Jack. I'm sure of it. You know as well as I do how smart she was. You might have missed it if you only knew her when she was drinking. Or sedated. But she was observant. She had the eye of an artist. I'm sure she had been in his unit and looked around. She probably heard him speaking on the phone. She probably saw people there who didn't look like health-care executives. Guzman could probably explain all of it, but your mother's bullshit meter was sensitive. And remember, she hadn't been drinking much or taking drugs for months now. She was as close to the top of her game as she was ever going to be."

I thought about this as I rolled bourbon around in my mouth. My own bullshit meter was pinging.

"I don't see it. Assuming what you are saying about him is true, Guzman didn't get where he is—juggling those two careers—by executing everyone who suspected he might be dirty. There would be a lot of bodies and a lot of unwanted attention. Guzman seems like a finesse guy."

"I think you're right about that, Jack. So add one more thing. Your mother was competitive. When she set a hook, she boated the fish. You've seen it yourself many times."

He paused for a long pull on his glass, finishing it with one swallow. He turned on his stool to face me.

"We've never talked about this directly, but I think you're smart enough to know that Betty was pregnant with your brother when we got married. Our anniversary and his birthday were a little too close not to be noticed. Maybe Betty talked to you about it. Personally, I have no regrets. I could never have wished for a better son than Bobby, but your mother eventually told me she had stopped using birth control right about the time I said yes to the Army. She had no intention of losing me to Uncle Sam and, as it turned out, she didn't."

He smiled wistfully as he ran through the images in his mind's eye.

"Believe it or not, I respected her resolve. I didn't see deception but a willingness to commit to a goal. And, as she pointed out, she owed me nothing at the time. We were not exactly exclusive and I wasn't insisting on condoms. So the point is, Betty hated to lose. So what if she wasn't willing to accept whatever Guzman was offering? She was committed to a divorce and he was committed to nothing. I don't think she cared much about the drugs. We both knew plenty of drug dealers in our lives. The percentage of assholes was about the same as in the general population and your mother was no hypocrite. But I don't think she was going to accept anything but a complete commitment from Guzman and this time there could be no pregnancy. So I think she blackmailed him. Not overtly, of course. That would be too crass for a Donovan. But I'd bet anything she started to hint at how much she knew, probably dropping little clues in group conversations just to gauge his reaction. I'm speculating, of course, but I really think I'm onto something. I can't stop going through it in my mind and I keep thinking it makes a lot more sense than suicide."

He stopped to pour more bourbon in our glasses. I waited for him to continue, but he seemed to have concluded his presentation. I tried to forget we were talking about the woman who raised me, who as far as I knew was alive just twelve hours ago, and thought about it clinically.

"So why not tell all of this to the police?"

"That's just it. I can't talk to the police about it without something solid. If I give them any reason to doubt it was a suicide, I'm going to look like a much better suspect than Guzman."

That startled me.

"What do you mean?"

"I mean everything I'm saying about Guzman is bullshit. With me, there's the divorce, which was going to be expensive. There's no pre-nup. And there's a two-million-dollar life insurance policy. Two million dollars doesn't buy what it used to, but it's still a lot of money, particularly to a homicide detective searching for a motive. But motive without means or opportunity is pretty flimsy."

He paused to take another swallow. I noticed a slight tremor in his index finger as he lifted his glass. Putting the glass down and self-consciously sticking his hand in his pocket, he continued.

"Unfortunately, I had both. Means and opportunity. I was there, Jack, I'm almost sure of it, right before she did it. I know no one saw or heard from her after I did, judging by her cell phone, which was right next to her. The police have that now but don't know about me. I told them nothing when I went over there. If they start looking past an obvious suicide, they're going to see my car coming and going on the garage security camera. If they pin the time of death close to my exit, which they will, I could have a problem."

I asked the looming question, "Why were you there in the first place?"

The Duke pondered what should have been easy, seemingly evaluating which cards to lay on the table. He shook his head.

"It was just a simple errand. I had been over there taking an expert's deposition on Alton Road and decided to swing by on my way back to the mainland to pick up my tuxedo, which I had never moved over here. I have the American Cancer Society fundraiser in a couple of weeks. I called ahead and got voicemail. I didn't even know if she was there. I still have a key. Whatever you might think, Jack, the divorce was not bitter. Our marriage was pretty much over after Bobby died. It was probably in trouble even before that, but afterward, we just didn't seem to be able to give what the other needed. There's plenty of blame, and I don't want to get too deep into it, but the point is we were both okay with splitting up."

He sounded convincing. But who was he trying to persuade? I hadn't been around much in those last years, but I never noticed them fighting when I was. Of course, my mother was in no shape for fighting during a lot of it. It was only after I was in Key West that I saw signs of her natural personality in her infrequent texts and emails. I winced at the thought of how few actual conversations I had with my mother during her last year.

The Duke noticed my discomfort and guessed at the source.

"Don't blame yourself, Jack. Your mother didn't make it easy for you when you left. She had a sharp tongue when she was drinking. I have to say I was a little surprised you didn't tell her about our arrangement. I could have handled whatever she had for me and was prepared to do it. But you spared me that for reasons I've never quite understood. As you know, I've always appreciated your loyalty. Both to me and your brother."

That earned a scornful grunt from me. The bourbon was loosening my tongue.

"It wasn't loyalty. To you, at least. It was penance. I deserved every bit of derision and scorn I got from her and everyone else who mattered in my life for not having the balls to put the truth up against the Duke. I might have lost—probably would have—but I'd feel a lot better about myself than I do right now sitting here looking at you."

Maybe that was true. I remembered it that way. Looking at it now, though, it probably always was a business transaction I preferred to keep quiet. But the Duke was observing me, always plotting behind those bottomless black eyes. He was deciding if this was new information and, if so, what to do with it. I think he decided it was bullshit.

"None of it matters now," he said. "The point is that there are good reasons for me not going to the police. But the best one is that I can't risk an autopsy, which would be automatic if her death were deemed suspicious."

He managed to surprise me again. "Now what are you talking about? Of course they're going to find drugs in her system."

"Not drugs. If they look, they're going to find semen—and that semen is going to have my DNA."

I gaped at him wordlessly. He returned the slightest hint of a rueful smile.

"You remember how it was with us, Jack. We always had the chemical attraction, no matter what else was going on. As I said, I didn't even know she was going to be home, but there she was. We started talking about things. We hadn't seen each other in a while and were mostly communicating through lawyers at that point. It felt good to talk and feel the electricity a little bit. Do you know what I'm talking about, Jack? Anyway, one thing led to another and the next thing I know, my cell phone rings a few days later and the police are telling me she committed suicide. So I'm having a hard time believing that's what happened. I just can't do anything about it. At least not officially."

"What about the press? Couldn't you feed this to a reporter and get an investigation going? Unofficially?"

"Hah! That would be a disaster. Guzman is much better thought of in the media than me. And if his connection to Betty's death didn't pan out, the only thing left would be the sex angle. Which I would have just handed over on a plate. That's not the headline anyone is ever going to read, Jack."

And there he stopped. I didn't have much to add, although my memory of what followed is vague, likely the result of the half-bottle of bourbon I had consumed. I know I had bottomed out, emotionally. The day's toll was being paid. I remember delivering some expletive-laden insults and accusations of infidelities I had only heard about after my launch from Miami had reached exit velocity. None of it had mattered much from the vantage of space. But as any astronaut will tell you, reentry is a bitch.

CHAPTER ELEVEN

I was awakened by a tentative knock—momentarily confused by unfamiliar surroundings amid the ravages of a two-day hangover. Marta's muffled voice from beyond the door reoriented me.

"*Buenos días, Jaquito. Tienes que desayunar, mi corazón.*"

I grumbled incoherently before managing a response.

"*Sí, sí. Lo siento. Tengo que duchar ahora mismo. Hay toallas?*"

"*Allí en el baño. Hasta pronto, Jaquito.*"

And with that, she padded off in her blessedly soft-soled shoes on the hardwood floor. I managed to lift myself up—slowly—and perched on the edge of the king-sized bed. I was wearing the clothes I arrived in and felt a little gamey. With Marta's offer of breakfast before me, I pulled myself all the way up and spotted a spacious bathroom through a doorway to the left of the bed where a hot shower awaited. Behind me, a floor-to-ceiling window provided a panorama of the canal, the park, and the bay I had never seen before, having never had this second-story point of view.

The sun was well up in the east, so I knew instinctively it was around ten a.m. I was a little surprised, although I shouldn't have been, to see the Duke idling along in the Contender on his return from an early morning on the bay. I watched as he expertly brought the boat to the dock, the hull barely kissing the bumpers. He obviously had no difficulty operating the big boat alone. I was again reminded of how much time all of us had spent puttering back and forth on that canal over the years. The Duke deftly hopped onto the dock, shirtless and shoeless, to secure the lines. Lean as ever, he appeared to be in fighting trim and feeling none of the effects I was. Did he trick me last night? I was sure we were drinking from the same bottle.

Giving this only a passing thought, I turned toward the bathroom and discovered the small gear bag I had packed before leaving home on a beautiful mahogany dresser that appeared to be an antique. I mused that for this to be one of the furnishings in a guest bedroom, the Duke's business was indeed prospering. With this and other thoughts arising from last night's discussion percolating in my mind, I proceeded to brush my teeth, shave, shower, and dress in faded jeans and a low-key blue print Tommy Bahama shirt. Having subdued yet another hangover—I was getting a little too good at this—I ventured out into the hallway and found the two-tiered open stairway to the ground floor. Walking into the large kitchen, I found Marta placing a plate of Cuban tostadas, scrambled eggs, and diced fried potatoes in front of the Duke, who now wore a loose white linen shirt as he sat on a stool at the center island. I could smell the café con leche steaming in the mug he was bringing to his lips. Putting the mug down as he saw me approach, his eyes surveyed me to assess the damage the night had wrought. He gave no indication of hard feelings resulting from things I said, or might have said.

"Good morning, Jack. Marta was worried about you."

He evidently harbored no such worries. Marta busied herself preparing a plate for me without comment.

"Well, Dad, a craftsman never blames his tools. I've become something of a professional and that was really good bourbon. I feel just fine."

This glib response was belied by the scratchy voice that delivered it. The Duke took note.

"As with many things, Jack, there's a time to press forward and a time to survey the disposition of the battlefield and realize it's time to pull back. There's no shame in it. You've always had a hard time with moderation."

He was probably right about that, but I saw no point in debating it. I did know the Duke was suggesting something beyond the four corners of the battlefield metaphor.

"So why don't you tell me about the black eye, Jack."

I should mention here that my new Navy friend Zeke had managed to catch me with an elbow to the cheek during our brief tussle at Jack's Hideaway. It was an inadvertent blow that I barely felt at the time. My cheek was slightly red and swollen, but by the next morning, my left eye was a little bloodshot and I knew a shiner was on the way. This may partially explain why everyone I had seen since Friday thought I looked like crap. Now, on Sunday, I had a nice little purple, yellow, and brown half-moon under my eye. It hardly seemed worth mentioning, but the Duke had apparently been politely waiting for me to explain it and now had lost patience.

"It was nothing. Just a little trouble with a customer."

Marta handed me a cup of café con leche with concern in her eyes, although she had seen worse damage to both Bobby and me over the years.

The Duke was evidently thinking along similar lines as he watched, stating, "Marta spent a lot of time patching you and your brother up over the years. Mostly your brother, now that I think of it. You two loved to fight."

Actually, we didn't. At least not with each other. But we were loyal and kept each other's secrets. Sitting on a stool next to my father, I thought about my brother as I reflexively pointed out, "Well, I was a lot bigger than Bobby."

The Duke thoughtfully munched on his eggs as his eyes drifted through the broad kitchen window to the dock and the boats moored there. My own thoughts circled back to the last two years of high school when my relationship with my brother violently shifted.

Both of us, from an early age and at the Duke's insistence, had been enrolled in martial arts classes, starting with a generic karate class at a strip mall dojo. The Duke himself had been trained in several disciplines focusing primarily on killing techniques while in the Army, but decided later that we should have broader training emphasizing self-defense and discipline. He eventually found what he was looking for in a man we came to know only as Mr. An.

Mr. An was a senior instructor in the Wing Chun style of Chinese kung fu and worked with a limited number of students in his home studio in West Miami. He was a small man in his fifties, gentle in speech, graceful in manner, and relentless in his quest for purity of mind. And he could pack a punch. For Bobby and me, the selling point was the martial artist and actor Bruce Lee, probably the most famous Wing Chun practitioner ever. Watching *Enter the Dragon* with our father was all we needed. Watching Lee and John Saxon team up in a fight against overwhelming numbers to achieve victory was potent stuff for two boys like us. We were in.

What was so attractive about the Wing Chun fighting style was its focus on a loose, relaxed, and upright posture, allowing an easy flow with an opponent's stiff and lumbering attacks. On offense, this permitted short, fast-moving blows to points down the center of the body, primarily the neck, chest, stomach, and groin. For Bobby and me, it was a blast from day one, and we always looked forward to our weekly sessions with Mr. An. Eventually, both of us worked our way through the ten levels of the open hand system of Wing Chun, earning our gold sashes by mastering advanced fighting and combat concepts. There were bruises and sprains along the way but, almost as an afterthought, Mr. An managed to instill in us some measure of the three fundamental values of kung fu: honesty, loyalty, and integrity. I've spent many sleepless nights since Bobby's death wishing he had not taken those values so seriously. Certainly, I had managed to compromise them. Our father never admitted it, and it would have crushed Bobby to know it, but the Duke recognized these values not as aspirational goals but as qualities to be manipulated in others. I realized this too late, but at least Bobby was spared.

As you can imagine, Bobby and I practiced and sparred with one another, inflicting regular damage ministered to by always-affectionate Marta and, to a lesser extent, our mother, who was never enthusiastic about this foray into our development as fighters. The Duke grimly noted our progress, encouraging us to continue but taking no apparent pleasure in it, instead insisting that we both memorize a seminal quote from Nietzsche, which, looking back, should have served as a warning: "Whoever fights monsters should see to it that in the process he does not become a monster. And if you gaze long enough into an abyss, the abyss will gaze back into you."

The Duke, we knew, had fought many monsters. We were unclear about the abyss.

Skillful as Bobby and I had become, we didn't have much practical experience fighting others in uncontrolled environments.

That changed, at least for Bobby, during our junior year. I came home from football practice one fall day to find Bobby in my room, sitting on the edge of the bed, apparently waiting for me. He was sporting a nasty split lower lip that made speaking painful. With a wince he said as I entered, "Just so you know, you did this."

"It's funny, Bob, but I don't remember that."

He pressed on, "We were practicing out back and you accidentally caught me with a knee."

"Still not ringing a bell."

"Look, Jack, no screwing around. I need you to cover for me with Mom. I don't think Dad would care, but Mom would freak."

"About what, Bobby? What's going on?"

"I just made $400 in about a minute and a half, Jack. That's what's going on."

And that's how it started. A guy we knew from Coral Gables High School, J.B. Watkins, had graduated the year before. His father was a local boxing promoter who was beginning to branch into mixed martial arts events. All of this was aboveboard and regulated by the state. J.B., however, was well aware of the sums of money being illegally bet at these otherwise legal events because his father had a sideline as a bookie and employed J.B. as a runner before the fights started. He could make up to a thousand dollars for a night's work if he hustled. And J.B. was a hustler. So much so that he decided to transfer his unique knowledge and skills to the very loosely organized and entirely unregulated world of bare-knuckle fighting as it existed in backyards and warehouses around Miami at the time.

J.B. began putting small events together by word of mouth and developed an eye for talent and an understanding of the existing pool of fighters. In a city where crowds of a thousand or more would gather to bet on a cockfight, he knew there was real money to be made pitting humans against one another in no-rules combat. I didn't know all of this at the time of that first confrontation with my brother, but it did seem out of character for him to participate in anything so dark, particularly for money. When he told me about J.B., I exploded.

"That asshole! How did he even know you could fight? And, now that I think of it, how the hell did he talk you into fighting? You can't possibly need the money."

Bobby's dark eyes shifted from mine and seemed to settle on a point on the floor beneath his feet. His voice barely more than a whisper, he said, "J.B. didn't know anything about me. I went to him and told him I wanted a fight. He put me off at first but I showed him one of the training videos we did with Mr. An. I guess he liked it because he told me he would pay me $400 guaranteed to fight a guy he had in mind—and that's what happened today. In the old dry storage barn at Dinner Key Marina."

He paused a moment before looking up at me to add, "I won."

I was familiar with the dry storage barn at the marina just north of our house. Bobby and I had worked summers there as dockhands at the Duke's urging, earning the minimum wage tending lines and washing boats for eight hours a day in ninety-degree heat.

"Jesus, Bobby, you've got to tell me why you did this. What the fuck? Were you trying to prove some point? Are you satisfied now?"

"I don't think so, little brother. And I don't think I owe you any more of an explanation. I'm just going to need you to run a little interference for me with our parents and Marta."

I fixed him with the strongest glare I could muster and said, "I don't want to lie to them, Bobby. This has to be really important."

Without blinking, he returned my stare and stated simply, "It is."

And that was enough for me. It marked the beginning of my career covering up for Girard men. I wondered about it from time to time over the next couple of years, particularly when he was a little more banged up than he was that first day, but it was only after he died that Bobby told me why he did it.

CHAPTER TWELVE

Back in the kitchen mindlessly picking at the eggs Marta had placed before me, I noticed that the Duke had turned to look at me, apparently sensing that we were through talking about Bobby.

"So after you've eaten, I'd like to take you over to the condo to look around. Maybe you'll notice something. The homicide cop really wasn't looking for anything. At least it seemed to me."

Unspoken here was his supposition that my experience with suicide might yield some insight refuting his murderous lover fantasy. The Duke was always practical and wouldn't want to waste time on a pipe dream, however much he wanted it to be true.

"Sure," I responded. "I wanted to see it either way. I was hoping I could find some meaning in it. Or maybe just understanding."

Pushing my plate away, I concluded, "Let's go."

The short drive across the causeway to Miami Beach in the Duke's Jaguar F-Pace SUV elapsed in near silence, the only sound being the muted purr of the powerful engine joined by the higher-pitched hum of the tires turning on the road surface. The Duke never listened to music—or anything else—while driving, content as he was to immerse himself in his own thoughts, wherever they led. I found myself gazing out the passenger-side window at the line of cruise ships moored at their berths along Government Cut, filling up with vacationers anxious for tropical adventure. Already, at one in the afternoon, the railings along the upper decks were dotted with people taking selfies against the riveting Miami skyline or imagining what was to come as they looked east out to sea. I envied them.

I was jarred from these thoughts by the Duke's right turn onto Alton Road, the condominium building looming ahead of us off South Pointe Drive. As we pulled up to the valet stand, I was prompted to ask, "When you stopped by to get your tuxedo, why didn't you just valet?"

From behind the wheel, the Duke studied me briefly, attempting to discern whether the question was a challenge. Opening the door and handing the keys to the attendant along with a ten dollar bill, he said as he rose, "I didn't have any money for a tip. I still have access to the garage so I went in and parked there. No big deal."

As I got out of the car, I noticed two security cameras scanning the circular drive from the corners of the portico shielding residents and guests from the weather. The Duke and I climbed the five steps to the front entrance in tandem and were greeted by the doorman, who held the steel and glass door open for us.

"Good afternoon, Mr. Girard."

He was a six-foot block of a man whose features seemed carved from ebony. His dark blue uniform was well cut, his white shirt starched, and maroon tie masterfully knotted. His face reflected uncertainty about whether to acknowledge the preceding tragedy. The Duke, noticing this, said, "Good afternoon, Jonathan. I know how difficult these last few days have been for you and the others here. Betty always spoke highly of you and your professionalism."

"She was a fine woman, sir."

"Yes, she was. Thank you. And this is our son, Jack. I don't think you've met."

Turning to me, he said, "Jack, please meet Jonathan. He's been on the security staff here since we bought the place." Stepping forward to shake my hand, Jonathan said, "I'm sorry to meet you like this, sir. You should know that your mother was a friend to all of us. We'll miss her."

Meeting his eyes and holding them as he released my hand, I said, "Thank you, Jonathan. I should have met you earlier. I'm sorry I didn't."

With nothing more to say, the Duke and I walked across the gray marble floor of the lobby to the elevator banks. Upon entering the open elevator, I looked up and saw that there were no security cameras inside the car. Turning to the Duke, I pointed and said, "That's kind of a security lapse, isn't it?"

Looking around, the Duke answered, "Probably. I think there were cameras at one point, but the residents didn't like it. This isn't a hotel. The number of people who actually use these elevators is pretty small and anyone coming from outside will show up on multiple cameras. Anyway, you can see how this might have helped someone wanting to go between floors unnoticed."

With that he glanced up at the floor numbers above the doors, serially lighting up as we ascended, ending in PH. Right. Guzman lived in the penthouse. And he didn't have a private elevator, which was an increasingly common feature in luxury condominiums. That might have been a security lapse on his part, I thought.

When the doors opened on seventeen, we stepped out onto the rich plum carpet lining the hallway and made our way to the door of my mother's last home. Pulling a key from his pocket, the Duke swiftly opened the door without hesitation and walked in. The corner unit had a large, open floor plan with floor-to-ceiling windows on two walls. The kitchen was to the immediate right and the dining room to the left. Two doorways along the left side of the unit presumably led to bedrooms while a great room featuring spectacular views of Biscayne Bay and Government Cut beckoned straight ahead. My mother's taste was everywhere, from the light bamboo floors to the soft pastel fabrics on the sofas and chairs. Along the wall of the great room separating her bedroom she had created something of a studio, with a commercial drafting table, easels, and canvases ranging in sizes and stages of completion. Fixed upon one easel, before which sat a paint-stained stool and a small table scattered with brushes and tubes of pigment, was a small work in progress. It was a portrait of a woman standing at the helm of a sailboat, feet planted firmly with eyes fixed forward. Her face was only sketched in, so I couldn't make out the color of her eyes or hair, but it was definitely not my mother. I also noticed there was no reference photograph, meaning that Betty was painting the subject from memory, imagination, or in person.

The Duke was still standing in the entrance foyer, watching me as I made my way through the room. Looking back at him, I asked, "Do you know who this is?"

"This isn't the first thing I thought we'd be talking about, Jack, but let me take a look," he said as he strode across the room. "I forget that you've never been here. Your mother was doing a lot of work over the last year or so."

Leaning in to examine the one-by-two-foot canvas, the Duke let out a long breath, jammed his right hand into the pocket of his shorts, and muttered, "Nope. I can't say I know this person. I guess it could be anyone. Or no one."

I thought about that as the Duke straightened. "I never knew Mom to paint a person without a model. She didn't have that sort of gift, to invent fully formed people."

"I'm sure you're right," responded the Duke. "But I don't know who this is."

Pausing for a moment as he stepped away, he added, "It does seem a little inconsistent to commit suicide with a half-finished portrait on your easel. Maybe you should take a look in her bedroom. See what you think."

I admit that I hadn't been giving the Duke's murder theory much credence. He was obviously pissed off about Julio Guzman, but his conjecture about why Guzman would deem it necessary to kill Betty seemed a little hysterical. But as I looked around, I didn't see finality. Aside from the unfinished portrait, there was an open, half-empty bottle of Evian water and a small white towel on a corner of the glass-topped dining room table, as if they had been haphazardly left there after a workout in the gym downstairs. There was a short stack of mail on the kitchen counter nearest the front door. There were unwashed dishes in the sink, including a wineglass still a quarter full. It seemed unlikely that a tidy person like my mother would depart leaving these things for others to deal with. With emerging doubt, I followed the Duke into the bedroom.

The first thing I confronted as I walked through the door was the unmade bed. Of course, I was forced to imagine the Duke and Betty together there on that final evening. Pushing that thought aside, I focused more on the fact that the bed was unmade. Betty would not have willingly gone out like that. If, for whatever reason, she was suicidal after her encounter with the Duke, she would have eliminated all traces of it. I was sure of that.

I noticed the Duke watching me, no expression on his face. He knew what I was thinking and wisely chose not to comment. Turning from the bed, I surveyed the room. The east wall featured floor-to-ceiling windows, including a bank of sliding glass opening onto a private balcony. Just inside the sliders against the wall next to the bed was my mother's antique cherrywood dressing table, an heirloom passed down to her through three generations of Donovans. A cushioned leather stool sat in front of the table and to the right, about three feet from where it ought to have been. Following my eyes and noting the question he found there, the Duke said, "That's where she was, Jack. She was sitting on the stool with her head in her arms on the table as if she were asleep. I saw it myself. They moved the stool when they took her out."

I felt my face flushing and my heart beginning to race. I thought of Bobby and felt shamefully glad I didn't find Betty. Moving toward the table, seemingly drawn to it by gravity, I took in the various cosmetics and perfumes, the makeup mirror, the box of tissues, and—here was the shock—Bobby's Mont Blanc fountain pen and the very same bottle of indigo ink I discovered in Bobby's room ten years before. I was sure of it. I didn't know shit about ink, but that fifty-milliliter cut glass bottle with the Iroshizuku Shin-Kai white label was forever etched in my brain. Moving the stool back to the table and sitting down, I tried to compose myself. The Duke had moved behind me, aware that I'd noticed something significant.

"What is it, Jack? What do you see?"

"Is this where the note was found? On this table?"

"Yes. The police took the note. What of it?"

"I have to see the note."

With a feeling of foreboding, I opened each of the three drawers on the right underside of the table. And there in the bottom drawer, empty of all other contents, I found a 4x6 photograph, a sheaf of pale-yellow stationery, and a single envelope with a document inside. I picked up the photograph, noticing that my hand was shaking slightly. To prevent the Duke from noticing this, I put the picture down on the table to look at it more closely. It was a snapshot of my mother and Bobby seated together on the transom of our boat with the Fowey Rocks Lighthouse in the background. The lighthouse was itself distinctive, with its octagonal pyramid shape, brown-painted cast-iron structure, and two-story living quarters situated halfway up its imposing 110-foot height. Bobby could not have been more than thirteen at the time, our mother's pale, slender arm wrapped protectively around his shoulders as he smiled contentedly into the camera. Betty's guileless blue eyes shone brightly in the sun, her damp blond hair falling haphazardly in the breeze. We had been to this popular spot southeast of Key Biscayne countless times, but I sensed there was something special about this particular cloudless day: it obviously meant something to Betty. Looking over my shoulder, the Duke recognized the photo immediately.

"You took that picture, Jack. That was the day Bobby finally stayed down on a free dive longer than your mother. We didn't time it, but it was over three minutes. She couldn't believe it. She blamed it on El Toro."

I reflexively laughed at the now vivid memory.

"Yep. She was pissed. She said she was startled by the shark, which Bobby never saw."

"Neither did you. Or me, although I was in the boat."

"Is El Toro still out there stealing people's fish?"

El Toro was a thirteen-foot male bull shark inhabiting the area around Fowey Light and farther north along Key Biscayne. Bull sharks are territorial, and this one was well known for snatching fish hooked by unsuspecting anglers as they reeled in what they hoped would be dinner. Experienced fishermen knew to waste no time getting fish to the boat in the event El Toro had sensed movement or blood.

"As far as I know, he is," replied the Duke. "Although I don't go down there much anymore. That was more of a place for the family."

Still looking at the picture, I said, "Those were good days. Mom swore she saw that shark."

"Who knows? Maybe she did."

Bull sharks, although fearsome in appearance with their thick bulk and toothy mouths adept at tearing into tuna and other large schooling fish, aren't much interested in humans and tend to keep them at a distance, even in their home territory. They will only attack humans in confusion, usually in poor visibility, which was never an issue on a sunny day in the crystal clear water around Fowey Light.

"Anyway," said the Duke, "that was a fond memory for your mother. Her oldest boy was growing up. I didn't know she kept that picture."

Looking back in the drawer, I replied, "That wasn't all she kept."

With increasing dread, I seized the envelope, certain before opening it that I had held it years before. Pulling out the single tri-folded sheet within, I noticed that the creases were relaxed, as though the page had been unfolded and refolded many times. Unfolded once again, I confronted my brother's words for the second time.

MOTHER, FATHER, BROTHER

I know the pain I'm causing you
    With the shortened life I'm leaving,
The pain I'd cause by remaining
    Would be deeper and unceasing.

As a child I often wondered
    About the person I would be,

My questions have all been answered,
    There's no more doubt about me.

So I've studied myself in the mirror,
    Is this friend or is it foe?
I can't square what I feel with the person I see,
    One of us has to go.

Please remember what I've been and not what I am.
I love you all

Heart pounding, jaw clenched, determined not to allow the welling tears in my eyes to fall, I sat and wondered if the pain of this lie had finally overwhelmed my mother. Torturing herself with the proof of it over and over, had she also reached an end? Was she unable to hold the gaze of the person looking back at her from the mirror atop this table? It seemed as likely as the spurned lover theory. Immersed in these thoughts, I'd forgotten about the Duke standing behind me.

"What is it, Jack? What's in the envelope?"

"It's Bobby's note. I really need to see Mom's."

"Bobby's note. What are you talking about?"

Incredulous, I turned to look at him.

"Bobby's suicide note." Waving the page in front of him, I said, "This is it. The original from the condo. She's kept it all these years right here."

The Duke looked at me quizzically.

"Wait, we talked about this. Bobby's death was an accident."

I was momentarily speechless at the enormity of what he said.

"I'm talking about reality, Dad. This is real. Mom never accepted the alternate version."

"Listen, Jack. Reality is a belief system. Reality for you is made up of all the things you believe in right now. Us standing here talking is real only because we're both experiencing it at the same time. But we'll recall it differently, right? Most of reality is shared by most people without a thought or need for convincing, but all of us consider any number of things to be real that aren't found in someone else's reality. Religion provides the easiest examples. But you can create reality for yourself, Jack, as long as it doesn't conflict too much with the reality experienced by too many others. For me, the reality is that Bobby's death was an accident. No one else's reality differs from that in any meaningful way. Your mother and I had a long talk about this at the time. I thought she eventually came to terms with it. I know I did."

I stared at him for a long moment, my brain still overloaded with emotion, adrenaline, and the aftereffects of alcohol.

"That is complete bullshit, Dad! There is objective reality. Bobby really did kill himself. I found him. Remember?"

"I'm not disputing what you're saying, Son, but you're missing my point. My reality simply doesn't include what you're saying. That's a choice I was able to make, and my life's been better for it. Your mother apparently chose a more confrontational approach. And it caused her endless pain, from the looks of it."

"Jesus, Dad! You can't heal if you never admit you're bleeding. Everyone has to find a way to face painful experiences and get over them."

"That's what's bullshit, Jack! And I know! I don't talk about Iraq, right? It's because most of that's gone for me. It's no longer real. Don't you see that if it were possible to surgically remove the neurons storing her belief in Bobby's suicide from Betty's brain, she would have nothing to get over? I believe it's possible to achieve the same thing with the right mindset, the right way of thinking."

I'd had enough.

"This is crazy talk, Dad. I'm not doing this now."

After a pause, I added, "You never even read Bobby's note, did you?"

"Why would I? It wasn't going to help me. I don't think it helped Betty. Or you."

Thrusting the note toward him, I ordered, "Read it! Now!"

With only the slightest hesitation, he took the note and began reading. His brow furrowed as he finished and looked up. By now, I had moved away and was standing near the sliding door, the kaleidoscopic azure and green surface of Biscayne Bay glistening in the winter sun behind me.

In a quiet voice, the Duke asked, "What does this mean, Jack?" I detected a tremor of emotion.

"Are you kidding? You actually don't know?"

"Know what, damn it? Why is my son dead?"

"Because he was gay! How could you not know that? Mom knew. I think she always knew. Didn't you talk about this?"

"With your mother? No! We weren't talking about why. We were talking about perspective. The right way to look at this so we could deal with it."

"So you were doing the talking. That I can see. I can also see Mom realizing there was no point in telling you. Nothing would change. Hurting you more wouldn't bring her son back. Jesus! She really was all alone."

The Duke wasn't having it.

"But this is ridiculous! Bobby wasn't gay! He hated gays!"

"No, *you* hated gays! You made that very clear to us growing up."

"I don't hate gays! Where did you get that? They just don't fit. They have no evolutionary purpose. They are one of nature's wrong turns. We should all just recognize that and do what we can to stop perpetuating it. That's all. I never said they weren't human or didn't have rights. Jesus, Jack!"

I'd heard this before, of course. So had Bobby. It was part of the naturalistic philosophical perspective the Duke had developed during college and fine-tuned in the hostile deserts of Iraq. He devoured the writings of Friedrich Nietzsche and was prone to inserting them in conversations. The basic premise the Duke made sure we understood was that humans were simply the current product of an ongoing evolutionary process, nothing more. The human process was different from that experienced by other animals, resulting in a consciousness that was capable of imagining things that weren't real. Those things—like God, for example—could be used to maintain social order. And order provided the true basis for human survival. The Duke despised conservative politicians and commentators who liked to quote Nietzsche on the need for strong social rules without embracing the atheism lying at the center of his thinking. They obviously hadn't read *Beyond Good and Evil*, but liked some of what they'd heard about it. Bobby and I had read it before we were old enough to drive.

So the Duke's thoughts about homosexuality were not based on religion, or, more broadly, on morality, but on reproductive efficiency. To a couple of adolescent boys hearing this, it felt a little hateful. At least disdainful. For me, this triggered nothing more than curiosity, which, ironically enough, led to some college-level research revealing a fairly robust scholarly debate about whether Nietzsche was himself gay. For Bobby, the issue became an existential one. Now, with the Duke's smug confidence confronting me directly, I couldn't resist the urge to hurt him.

"You taught your son to understand that the life he finally realized he was living had no value. That's what you did. That's what's real. Now you just have to live with it."

With that, I walked out of the bedroom, leaving the Duke looking down at Bobby's note, undoubtedly trying to conjure an alternative reality. In the great room, I found myself standing next to the unfinished portrait on my mother's easel. The background action of the churning sea was rendered in bright shades of turquoise, emerald green, and creamy gold. There was vitality in the brushstrokes. Life. I really needed to see my mother's note.

After a few minutes, the Duke came out of the bedroom, empty-handed and composed as ever.

"Time to go, Jack. Unless there's more you want to see."

"No, I think I've seen enough."

CHAPTER THIRTEEN

The drive back to Rockerman Road was uncomfortably silent. There were obvious things a father and son should have talked about, but neither of us was inclined to initiate conversation. Keeping thoughts—and feelings—out of sight was a trademark of male Girards. Betty was different. She did her best to draw us out, but I knew she was frustrated in the attempt, particularly in her later years. I wondered if she thought she failed Bobby. Although she was a lapsed Catholic, guilt played a part in Betty's story, I knew. I wish I could talk to her about it now. I know a little about guilt.

The Duke's blithe dismissal of Bobby's suicide continued to eat at me. I was uncomfortably reminded of an approach to juries I had developed during my still nascent career as a trial lawyer. As a way of handling slight differences in witness testimony I knew were coming, I would remind jurors during my opening statement that what they would be hearing and seeing were recollections of events that occurred in the past; there would be no video of what transpired between the plaintiff and the accused defendant, as possibly observed by any number of people. Memories of the events, which typically occurred at least two years before, were understandably imperfect. What was important was the clarity of the bigger picture, not the smallest details. I would close this part of the speech with something like: "We're going to shoot for perfection—or truth. But in the end what we'll have is justice. Of that I assure you." Was I edging toward a malleable view of the past, similar to the Duke's? How much of a recollection had to be accurate to count as "true"? How far could you push it and still have justice? I didn't have that answer. I still don't.

Upon arrival at Rockerman Road, Marta was cheerfully waiting in the entrance hall in her smart khaki uniform, holding a tray with two tall glasses and a crystal pitcher containing, to my practiced eye, mai tais. Perfect. After leaning down to kiss Marta on the cheek, I seized the pitcher and poured about twelve ounces into a glass. Behind me, the Duke said, "Just one for me. I have a big day tomorrow and the service is on Tuesday. I'm going to do some work in my study. Jack, what about you?"

"More than one for me, Marta," I said with a smile I didn't feel. "I'm going to call down to Key West and then maybe watch the Eagles and Saints playoff game. I think it's at four thirty."

I handed the first glass to the Duke and proceeded to fill the second. Over my shoulder I asked, "Is there a TV room or something? I did notice a TV in my guest room, but I never turned it on."

"Let me show you to the game room. It's right there on the other side of the kitchen."

Leading me through the kitchen to the opposite doorway, the Duke paused and turned, almost causing me to spill my drink. Looking me hard in the eye, he said, "We'll speak no more of your brother. Do you understand me?" His black eyes searched my face for signs of comprehension.

"I do," I said after giving it some thought. This was a Girard conversation that had ended, as had many before it.

The Duke nodded and said, "What's important now is your mother. The service is Tuesday. I talked to her lawyer on Friday, and he told me she wanted her ashes spread at sunrise on the water by Fowey Light. I understand that now. You and I will do it on Saturday. Any problem?"

"None. I'm going back to Key West right after the service on Tuesday. I have a hearing in a case there on Wednesday afternoon. I'll come back on Friday."

The Duke's expression reflected curiosity about the case I was handling. I expected him to ask about it for the purpose of lampooning the waste of my talents, but he held his tongue. Turning again to lead me through the doorway, he simply said, "Good. The long-term forecast is not too bad. It'll be breezy."

We entered a surprisingly bright and open room featuring blond wood furniture covered in deep beige leather, an elegant carved-wood based pool table, a wet bar with four leather-topped stools, and a massive flat-screen TV dominating the rear wall facing the seating area. A poker table with six chairs was positioned near the floor-to-ceiling windows giving way to the terrace, pool, and dock. Two ceiling fans with blades shaped like palm fronds turned languidly overhead. The Duke pointed at the seating area and said, "The remote is on the table. It's the same cable lineup as you have in Key West, so you'll have no problem. There's booze and ice behind the bar. I'll leave you to it. I'm going to have dinner with a medical expert at Joe's Stone Crab, so you're on your own. Marta is probably already planning what to feed you."

On cue, Marta came through the door with the pitcher of mai tais and set it on the bar. Turning toward me with her hands clasped behind her, she said, "Please, Jaquito, unless you have special plans, let me cook something nice for you."

"I have no plans, Marta. That sounds great. Could we target around eight? The game should be over by then."

"*Perfecto, Jaquito.*"

With that she scurried out smiling. After a moment, the Duke turned to leave, saying over his shoulder, "Your mother didn't commit suicide, Jack. Not in any reality."

Under my breath to his retreating back I mumbled, "You may be right about that."

With some time before the game started, I decided to call Tracy at Jack's Hideaway to check in on Reggae Sunday. She would be irritated, but I needed to move my thoughts away from what I had discovered in my mother's condo. I had learned over the years to trust my subconscious mind to sort things out while I wasn't pondering them directly, often leading to a clear course of action when I raised them to the surface once again. Sitting down on the eight-foot sofa in front of the TV, I set my drink on the glass-topped coffee table and pulled my cell phone from the pocket of my shorts. Calling the number at the bar gave me a pang of longing to actually be there. Tracy picked up on the third ring.

"Jack's Hideaway. Tracy speaking. How can I help you?"

I could hear reggae guitar rhythms and crowd noise in the background, literally music to my ears.

"It sounds like you have a party going on, Tracy."

"Jack! Yes, we're having a good day . . . Wait a minute. Why are you calling? You don't trust me anymore?"

"Of course I do, Tracy. I won't even ask you who's working or what the sales look like. I just want to give you an update on my schedule."

"Oh. Okay. When do we have the pleasure of your return?"

I could see her smiling, pulling at her hair with her free hand. Lowering my voice and wishing I had made this call from my room, I said, "I'll be back on Wednesday afternoon or evening. I have a few things to do here."

"Sounds good. See you then. And don't worry about anything . . . Oh, Jack, wait, one other thing. The woman you were drinking with Friday night came in again last night."

Tracy's voice had taken on an accusatory tone.

"Okay, what about it?"

"She was alone and didn't order anything. She asked for you. I don't know, but she seemed a little upset."

This brought me to my feet. I was probably a little louder than I intended.

"Is that it? Did she say what it was about?"

"Take it easy, Jack. That was it. She just asked me to tell you she was here. Which I'm doing. Do you have her number?"

"No, and she doesn't have mine. Tracy, if you see her again, please give her my number. Okay?"

"Got it. Will do, Jack."

The music in the background stopped. Tracy said, "Listen, the band just went on break, so I have to go. The dancers are heading for the bar."

"No problem, Tracy. I'll see you soon."

The call ended there. Now I had something new to think about, but my primary concern was whether I had been overheard saying that I would return on Wednesday. I had decided on the drive back from Miami Beach that I wanted to look into a few things without input or interference from the Duke. I was going to make some calls on Monday and then follow up on Tuesday, or possibly Wednesday. I really did have a hearing in Key West, but it wasn't until Thursday afternoon and required little preparation. It occurred to me that the Duke might actually check that, but I dismissed the thought. He had no reason to question it, right?

I then debated calling my grandparents. Or at least my grandmother. I knew my grandfather was still on the course at Riviera on this fine Sunday afternoon. These Donovans were ritualistic creatures of habit who never varied absent a calamity. The unseemly death of an outcast daughter wouldn't qualify. I decided to make the call. When I heard my grandmother's thin, aging voice exclaim "Jack!" upon answering the recognized number, I couldn't help but wish I was there right then to wrap my arms around her. I knew how devastating this loss was for her, no matter the brave face demanded by her husband.

"I'm so sorry, Gram. I haven't really gotten a handle on it myself at this point."

"Oh, Jack! They say it was a suicide. I just can't believe it. I hadn't seen Betty in quite some time but I never would have thought it would come to this. Your grandfather says this is what happens to atheists."

As gently as I could, I said, "She wasn't an atheist, Gram. She just couldn't be a Catholic anymore. Is it still so hard to accept?"

"Your grandfather says that by renouncing the one true church she turned her back on God. And now she's paying for it."

"What about you, Gram? What do you say?"

"I don't know what to say, Jack. I feel such a weight pressing down on me I'm not sure I won't collapse! I keep thinking of Betty as a young girl. So happy and cheerful. She couldn't stop smiling. It was like she knew a special secret she couldn't share."

I could hear her voice trembling and could imagine the tears welling in the gray eyes that had seen so much.

"She did know a secret, Gram. She did. It just took her a long time to realize the price of keeping it. Maybe she let it go, but I don't believe she wanted to die."

"What are you saying, Jack? There was a note."

"I know, Gram. I don't know what I'm saying."

Changing the subject, I asked, "Can I come and see you, Gram? I feel like I should see you."

"Oh, I'd love to see you, Jack! But I don't think this is a good time. Your grandfather isn't handling this well, and I don't want you to see him this way. He's so . . . angry. It's hard to be around him."

I could feel the emotions pulling at her. Her daughter was dead. Her husband was deflecting the blow to avoid dealing with it, lashing out like a gravely wounded lion. Her grandson was offering much needed support, but her instinct to protect trumped all.

"I think I understand. I'd probably say something to make it worse anyway. I'm feeling a little defensive about Mom and I'm not sure I'm in complete control of myself."

"Well, how could you be? This is such a senseless, horrible thing."

"You're right, Gram. And I need to make some sense of it, that much I know. I'll call you again soon, and we'll just take it a step at a time with Gramps. Remember I love you and I'm here for you anytime."

"I love you so much, Jack! You're all I have now."

The implications of that felt like another knife wound. I hated the thought that it was true. Sooner or later, my grandfather and I were going to have to talk.

After ending the call, I reached for my drink and drained the glass in two long swallows. I was drinking too much but didn't feel inclined to stop. I got up and went to the bar to refill my glass, hesitating only for a brief moment before seizing the whole pitcher and taking it back to the couch. I turned on the TV and absently watched Drew Brees shred the Eagles' secondary. Before long the mai tais were gone, and I was back at the bar, switching to straight bourbon. Things got a little hazy after that, but I remember sitting with Marta at the kitchen table, eating arroz con pollo with fried plantains. Marta's concerned expression left more of an impression than any words we exchanged.

Eventually crawling into bed, I had one overriding thought: *Jack, you need to get your shit together.*

CHAPTER FOURTEEN

When I woke up, it was still dark. The luminous dial on my dive watch told me it was a little after six a.m. I felt a little better than I did the previous two mornings, meaning only that my system was adjusting to the nightly assaults with alcohol. I'd been drinking more than I should have since I moved to Key West, but I managed to avoid what—to me—would have been problem drinking by a fairly strict routine of running and weight-lifting. A three-night bender like the one I was on was unusual. Thinking that I needed to work up a sweat somehow, I put on the training shorts, tee shirt, and running shoes I had packed in my bag and headed for the stairs. As I descended, I heard the faint clatter of a cup and saucer and the tines of a fork on a plate. I knew I would find the Duke in the kitchen, immaculately dressed in a Brioni suit, crisp white shirt, and impeccably knotted silk tie. I was right. As I rounded the corner into the kitchen, the Duke looked up from the front page of the *Wall Street Journal* in mock surprise.

"Well, well. Is the early bird in search of a worm?"

I wasn't exactly sure how to take that, so I deflected.

"Actually, I was wondering if you have some sort of a home gym around here. I really need to work out."

I thought I saw the Duke internally debating whether to more explicitly pursue his original question, but he let it go.

"Of course, Son. I was using it a bit earlier. It's over on the other side of the house facing the pool. If you just go out the patio door and turn left, you'll find it toward the end. There's a bench, an Olympic bar, free weights, dumbbells, and a Smith machine including pull-up bars. You should be right at home."

Pausing for a moment, he observed, "You look to be in decent shape, at least from the neck down. How's your weight?"

"Still 205. My college weight, give or take." Eyeing him, I added, "How's yours?"

Smiling, the Duke responded, "I'm at 172 as of this morning. The exact same as when I landed in Qatar, ready to fight."

The look in his eyes didn't match his smile. The Duke always projected physical menace and was letting me know, as alpha males often do as a matter of reflex, that our size difference would make no difference if it came down to it. I had never been in any sort of physical conflict with the Duke and had never even wondered about the outcome. Who thinks about beating up his own father? One thing was not in doubt, though: the Duke would hold nothing back in a fight.

Turning to the coffeemaker sitting on the opposite counter, I poured a cup and stirred in some Sweet 'N Low and cream. Maybe it was too early in the morning, or maybe my hangover was affecting me, but I couldn't quite understand the tension in the room. I could feel the Duke pressing on me. Unwilling to pursue it, I turned back and said, "Well, I guess I'll get to it. Will you be back here later?"

The Duke hesitated. Clearly, he had more to say but chose not to say it.

"I'm not sure. We'll see how the day goes. Either way, remember we're meeting at Plymouth Congregational at ten tomorrow. If you look in the closet of your room, you'll find some of your old suits and ties. That's why I was asking about your weight."

I doubted that. He had been testing me. Why, I wasn't sure. And I didn't care just then. That might have been a mistake. Regardless, I responded, "Okay, great. I'm sure they'll fit. I'll let Marta know if there are any problems. Have a good one." And with that I carried my coffee out of the kitchen and turned toward the patio doors.

After a hard ninety-minute workout in the gym, I went for a four-mile run on a familiar course skirting the water along Bayshore Drive, winding through Coconut Grove along Tigertail Avenue, and then returning to Rockerman Road. It was a beautiful winter day, brisk and cloudless. While running, I allowed my thoughts to wander as I settled into a steady pace. I was having trouble identifying a rational reason why anyone else would want to kill my mother. There was no doubt she took the pills that killed her, and there was no sign of struggle. Was this a murder or a choice? If a choice, was it a free choice? If not a free choice, who set the price? Arriving back at the house, I was no closer to answers than I was when I started. The Duke's apparent conviction about Julio Guzman was significant. The Duke didn't draw idle conclusions. I was also troubled by my mother's apartment, particularly the unfinished painting. The vibrancy of the brushwork and the interplay of the colors were affecting. It didn't feel like the uncompleted act of a woman contemplating death. And, as the Duke mentioned, Betty hadn't been drinking for months. But the preliminary tox screen included alcohol, as further evidenced by the wineglass in the sink. What changed? Obviously,

I needed more information, and to get it I would have to make some calls, one of which, if it became necessary, I dreaded.

After showering and shaving, I felt better than I had in days. I was relaxed, and my mind was clear. I intended to keep it that way, given what I knew was coming. Dressed in jeans and a blue pinpoint Oxford dress shirt I found in the closet with the clothes the Duke had gathered for me, I skipped downstairs and found Marta in the kitchen. Her worried expression upon seeing me was disarming.

"Marta, please don't worry about me. You won't see a repeat performance of last night. Ever."

"Oh, Jaquito, I hate to see you grieving so. The pain this family has suffered—"

Cutting her off I said, "Marta, I know there is grief in it, but I think more than that I've been feeling sorry for myself. For a long time. That part is over now. I want my mother and my brother to be proud of me. It's time to stand up to my full height."

Hearing this, Marta burst into tears and threw herself against my chest, wrapping her arms around me and squeezing as hard as she could. I held her there for what seemed like a long time before her sobbing stopped. She looked up at me with her kind almond eyes, red at the edges, and whispered, "*Todos te queremos, Jaquito.* We were always proud of you, no matter what they said."

With all the love I could muster, I held her eyes steadily and replied, "*Gracias, Mamita.* You're the only one that never doubted me. Except maybe my father."

Marta didn't have any reason to catch the implication of that last part, nodding her head and saying, "Your father loves you, Jaquito. Always."

Rather than start a discussion of how my father assigned meaning to the word "love," I released her gently and changed the subject. The condo bedroom nagged at me. I wanted to find out what she knew about the most recent status of my parents' relationship, but I couldn't bring myself to put her in an uncomfortable position. She loved my mother when we were a family, but she had stayed with the Duke when the divorce started. It would be unfair for me to peel away the layers of loyalty in someone who had been so good to me. So instead, I simply asked, "Marta, do you think you could whip up one of your famous frittatas? I've worked up an appetite. And maybe a cafecito to get started? I'm going to be a little busy today."

Marta gave me a long look, knowing I was steering away from family issues but unsure of which ones. Accepting my choice, she said, "*Seguro, Jaquito.* Just give me ten minutes." With a smile she turned and headed for the espresso maker as I settled onto a stool at the center island where I had encountered the Duke earlier. Thinking of the Duke made me ponder the gravity of what I was planning. I was convinced that I needed to know more about my mother's death, but I hadn't thought much about what "more" meant or where it might lead. Even then, sipping on the perfectly sweetened cafecito Marta had placed in front of me, I couldn't envision the doors that might open with each revelation. Had I thought that all the way through, I would have done things differently.

CHAPTER FIFTEEN

Although of ordinary stature, Steve Amos was possessed of extraordinary skills. After a twenty-year career as a special agent in an FBI counterintelligence unit, he had joined Duke Girard & Associates as the titular head of investigations. Technically, he was to be consulted on any factual investigation undertaken by anyone, including the attorneys. He was very comfortable with both computer hardware and software technology and could usually find a shortcut to documentary information held virtually anywhere. In cases where criminal records were needed, his contacts in state, local, and federal agencies, including the DEA and CIA, were invaluable. In most of these instances the records at issue were subject to discovery by way of subpoena or public records request, but it was much more efficient to draft a subpoena covering records you already knew existed thanks to Steve's tenacious digging.

As a junior associate at the firm, Steve opened my eyes to the extraordinary volume of information pharmaceutical companies and their counterparts at various levels of government tried to shield from public scrutiny. Gaining access to this information was another way Duke Girard & Associates separated itself from competitors and generated huge windfalls for its clients, not to mention for the firm itself. As a result, Steve Amos was highly valued by the Duke, making as much in five years as he had in twenty with the FBI. Because I was the Duke's son, Steve patiently answered my questions and taught me how to organize an investigation, however big or small.

And so it was that I dialed Steve's direct line at the office as I stood looking out my window at the swaying fronds of the coconut palms across the canal in Kennedy Park. Marta was downstairs cleaning up the kitchen. The Duke had gone to work, and I briefly mused about the possibility that he was standing in Steve's office when the phone rang.

"Steve Amos," he announced with typical vigor when he picked up.

"Hi, Steve. It's Jack Girard. It's been a while."

Steve paused as he considered multiple responses, including, probably, hanging up. Eventually, he said, "Jack Girard. I've actually been thinking about you the last few days. It doesn't help much, I know, but I'm sorry about your mother. I didn't know her very well, but the news was still a shock. I can't imagine what you must be feeling."

"Well, Steve, that's just it. Aside from the loss itself, I'm not exactly sure how to feel. I'd actually like to talk to you about it. Off the phone."

Another pause. More options assessed.

"What do you have in mind, Jack?"

"How about a late lunch? Green Street Café at one."

"Well . . . okay. We can catch up. What's it been, two years? Three years?"

"Something like that. I'll see you soon."

After disconnecting, I thought about it from Steve's perspective. He had a perfectly legitimate reason for seeing me, a former colleague with whom he had a close relationship, as work relationships go. So there was no need to inform the Duke of the meeting in advance. If anything came of it, he would be free to tell the Duke all of it. As far as I could tell, the only useful thing arising from our conversation would be the fact that I was asking questions at all. And, as I thought about it, I didn't mind if the Duke found out about that.

With more than two hours before I had to make the short trip to the restaurant, I decided to take a shot at getting a look at my mother's note through the police ostensibly investigating the case. After initially reaching the Miami Beach Police Department, I found myself on hold for a few minutes before being connected to the Evidence Section. An officer whose name I didn't quite catch listened to my request and asked me to wait a moment while he checked the file. I heard the clicking on his keyboard along with his measured breathing. I wished he had just put me on hold while he did his thing. Finally, after clearing his throat, he cheerfully told me that my mother's note was marked "hold" by the investigating officer and could not be released until the investigation was over or the hold removed. He was unimpressed by the fact that it was my mother's note we were talking about and that I didn't want to remove it—I just wanted to see it. He wasn't budging, having come to a firm bureaucratic conclusion, so before frustration turned to anger, I thanked him for his time and hung up.

I still had over an hour before I had to meet Amos. Already feeling dejected, I decided to punish myself further with the call I could easily put off but which now seemed necessary. With a finite amount of time available, I would have an excuse to end it if things got uncomfortable. And who knew? Maybe she was already out to lunch. Punching in the number from memory, I could feel my hands getting clammy. Her caller ID wouldn't recognize this phone so there was a reasonable chance she would answer. She did.

"This is Detective Kaplan. How can I help you?"

She had one of those soft melodic voices that got me every time. It belied what I knew to be her iron-plated disposition and rigid drive to succeed.

"Hi, Lauren. It's Jack. I wouldn't call you if it wasn't important. Do you have a minute?"

I tried to keep my tone light but urgent. I hadn't spoken to Lauren Kaplan since I moved to Key West and was pretty sure she was glad about that.

"Jack."

She said it as a complete sentence, as if she were internally sorting through all of its implications. I jumped ahead.

"Lauren, I know you made things pretty clear when I was suspended, and I've respected that, but I need a favor. It's not a big deal, but I'll totally understand if you say no."

As she hesitated, I could picture her sitting at her desk, silky black hair pulled back in a ponytail, fierce ebony eyes setting fire to whatever paperwork lay in front of her. Lauren defined intensity. I hadn't quite understood that when I first met her in law school.

We had been in the same class of two hundred students but in different sections, meaning that we didn't actually share classes in the first-year curriculum. But we would see each other in the courtyard or in the cafeteria, exchanging the looks of people with sparked interest but no commitment to making a first move. For my part, I was instantly attracted to her tall, angular physique and confident, fluid way of moving. But I was still emotionally absent after the loss of my brother and subsequent breakup with my girlfriend. So I never mustered the energy to introduce myself. Before I knew it, she was gone.

I learned later that she had started law school with the intention of becoming a criminal prosecutor but realized almost immediately that becoming a lawyer would leave her too far from the action. She dropped out after the first semester and joined the City of Miami Police Department, finishing first in her academy class and earning her detective shield in record time. Which is when our paths crossed again at a holiday party for the County judges sponsored by the Duke and several other prominent local law firms. This time, two years into my career at Duke Girard & Associates, I didn't hesitate. Spotting her at the bar set up in a corner of the hotel ballroom, I walked up beside her and said, as smoothly as I could, "Law school was less interesting without you." She turned with the apparent intention of saying something disarming but stopped when the light of recognition turned on. Instead, she said, "You're Jack Girard," with a hint of wonder at the serendipity of the moment.

And that's where the most important—though short-lived—relationship of my life started. It took no time for us to realize the alignment of our interests in sports of all kinds, particularly on the water. The apex of our adventures was a single night on a dive trip to the Seven Mile Beach in Grand Cayman when, after an afternoon on the sand, Lauren rolled over and mischievously said, "Let's do a night dive."

Assuming she meant we would sign up with the local dive boat operator we had already been using for a guided nighttime tour of one of the many pristine deep-water reefs, I quickly responded, "Sure."

But that's not what she had in mind. Instead, we rented air cylinders from the dive shop in the hotel and ocean kayaks from a concessionaire next door. As experienced divers, we had brought all of our own dive gear, including powerful handheld halogen lights. Then, after the sun had long since set and the black sky was covered by a blanket of stars, we dragged our gear and kayaks to the water's edge and gazed out at the calm, dark water. A large half-moon seemed to light a path directly to the west. Turning to look at me without a trace of fear, Lauren said, "Are you ready, Jack?"

"As I'll ever be, Lauren," I replied.

And we were off. Fortunately, the reefs near the Seven Mile Beach are within two miles of the sand. Using my Garmin GPS dive watch, I led the way out to the dive site known as Big Tunnel, which starts out in sixty to seventy feet of water but descends through a long coral archway to about one hundred feet, at which point you are positioned along a wall that drops straight down to over a thousand feet. We had done this dive earlier in the trip in daylight and were exhilarated by it. Now, I was secretly terrified of navigating that inky blackness with only my light to guide me. What we were doing was not only crazy but illegal. But I could hear Lauren calmly paddling alongside me, and I could imagine the hint of a smile on her lips as she tested and exceeded yet another limit.

Once we were tied to the mooring buoy and geared up, Lauren reached across the bow of her kayak to squeeze my hand before wordlessly rolling over backward into the water. No turning back. I slid out of the kayak and oriented myself to Lauren's light. Everything else was pitch black. It's impossible to suppress your heart rate and breathing in these circumstances; the best you can do is maintain awareness of both and consciously choose to be calm. It doesn't work, but it limits the spikes. It's also impossible not to think about sharks, which are night feeders. But my own experience had been that sharks were put off by dive lights. So it was with a strong cocktail of excitement, adrenaline, and fear in my system that I followed Lauren deeper and deeper toward the looming reef.

Afterward, lying in bed giggling like children as we recounted the things we had seen—the startled barracuda that struck my face mask in its rush to escape, the bright oranges and reds of the majestic coral stands, the electric green of an illuminated moray eel easing back into its hole, the graceful swaying tails of two large sharks casually exiting the strangely lit scene—we seemed to be feeling the same sensory rush at the same time. I pulled her near me and held her silently for minutes that seemed like hours, aware in those minutes that I had never felt such peace, such serenity, in my life to that point. Looking into her eyes I believed she felt something similar, but when we kissed, tenderly at first and then passionately, I was sure.

It didn't last. In the fallout of my professional disgrace, Lauren zeroed in on a fundamental problem. Although dating a suspended lawyer did her career no favors, my refusal to challenge the Duke was unacceptable. Despite my brief outline of the futility of the fight and the consequences of a loss, Lauren believed I was simply afraid, which she couldn't tolerate. It was no accident that *Don Quixote* was her favorite novel. Of course, it's true that I was afraid, but my reasoning was a bit more nuanced than that. Where I saw a rational resolution of a many-sided problem, she saw weakness. Perhaps fueled by my own incipient self-loathing, I saw no reason to convince her otherwise. The die had been cast.

So now I wondered if any of this passed through her mind as she hesitated to speak on the phone. She finally said, "You hurt me, Jack. I didn't think you would just walk away."

That was not what I expected.

"Lauren, you were very clear about your feelings."

"I think you don't know enough about women."

Of that I was certain, but a discussion seemed pointless. I pushed ahead.

"Lauren, you probably know about my mother. It's been in the news. The Miami Beach Police have the file pending the ME's report. The Duke has persuaded the ME not to perform a complete autopsy under the circumstances, but there are tests being done before the final report is issued and the personal things collected at the scene are released. One of those things is the suicide note. I really need to see it. I was wondering if you could—"

She interrupted me, saying, "I'm not taking evidence out of an open investigation file, Jack."

"Of course. I'm not asking that. If you could just have the detective in charge take a picture of it and send it to you, you could then pass it along to me. Everyone then erases the picture from their phones like it never happened. I just need to see the note and I can't wait a week."

After a pause, Lauren said, "What's going on, Jack? Do you think this is something other than a suicide?"

Not wanting to lie to her, I said, "I think there may be something about Bobby in there. The service is tomorrow, and I want to know what it is before then. It's just personal, Lauren."

All of which was true. Mentioning my brother softened her.

"Okay, Jack. I'm pretty sure I can do it. Did you try asking for it yourself?"

"I did. It was a no-go. The clerk in the Evidence Section said the document was in the 'hold' category and couldn't be released until the investigation was over. He was pretty adamant. I really don't want to talk to the investigating officer because I know the Duke already did—and I don't want my inquiry getting back to him. I would bet the detective would call him the second he hung up with me. And I really don't want to talk to the Duke about my mother and Bobby anymore."

I guess I had raised my voice a bit because Lauren was silent for a moment, thinking about it.

"Despite everything, I really hope you work things out with your father. It's just the two of you now. At some point, the past has to be buried under the weight of all that's followed. It's his loss, too."

"I know. I'm sure there will be a time for us to resolve things. I think he's actually been trying to talk to me the last couple of days, but I've stayed away from the hard stuff. Anyway, I really appreciate your doing this, and . . ."

"And what, Jack?"

"I'm sorry, Lauren. I don't think I ever said that. I didn't think I was wrong back then. But even that was beside the point when it came to me and you."

"You're right about that, Jack. And I was a little too rigid on the wrong and right. I know that now."

Before I could respond, she said, "I'll talk to you soon."

And she disconnected.

Still standing at the window in my room, I glanced at the silent phone in my hand and tossed it onto the bed behind me. Looking eastward along the canal to the mottled blue bay beyond, sparkling in the tropical sun, I marveled at the pain this beautiful city had caused me. And it wasn't done yet.

In keeping with my new fitness resolution, I decided to walk the mile or so to the Green Street Café in the heart of the Grove. It was a perfect day, temperature in the seventies, low humidity and breezy. Walking on the shaded bike path along South Bayshore Drive, I was struck by the number of condominium and commercial buildings that had replaced the historic mansions perched on the western bluff of the coral ridge bordering the bay. So much had changed since I was a child skateboarding on the paths in Kennedy Park. The dense traffic on the once meandering two-lane road suggested the trade that was made for increased tax revenue. But I was detached from these issues now. As I passed the Coral Reef Yacht Club, I thought of my mother's childhood and the happy years she spent there learning to sail and developing the love for the bay and the ocean she instilled in all three males in her life, starting with the Duke. I wondered again about the painting in her apartment and what it meant beyond what it depicted. As I came upon the restaurant on Main Highway, I had a vague notion that it was about joy, or soul-deep satisfaction. If only she had filled in the woman's expression . . .

These thoughts were disrupted by the sight of Steve Amos seated at an outdoor table set up on the red brick sidewalk outside the café. He wore his typical creased khaki slacks and a red and green plaid short-sleeved shirt with button-down collar neatly tucked in around his still-trim waist. Seeing me coming, he stood up, and a broad smile crossed his distinctive face. Steve's gene pool was more of a mosh pit, as revealed by the narrowing of his eyes as he smiled and the creamy cappuccino tone of his skin, all reflective of the Asian, African, and Caucasian branches of his family tree. Steve and I never discussed his background—I only knew he was married by the slim gold ring he wore—although he certainly knew a bit about mine.

"Hello, Jack. I don't think I've ever seen you not wearing a suit."

He reached out to shake my hand. Grasping his, I chuckled and said, "It pretty much requires a court order to get me into a suit these days."

"How have you been?"

"Probably about the same as you remember. Let's sit."

Sitting down at the small umbrella-shaded table, I noticed that all ten of the outdoor tables were full, mostly tourists chattering away in the artificially upbeat way tourists do. Steve cut to the chase.

"It's good to see you, but I really doubt I have anything to tell you that your father couldn't."

"Maybe so, Steve, but I'd just as soon hear it from you. The Duke's motives sometimes elude me."

"Jack, I want you to know that I never knew anything about what came between you and the Duke. All of that computer work was between him and his assistant, and even now I don't know exactly what happened."

I eyed him levelly and said, "It wouldn't have been hard for you to find out exactly what happened and who did what, though, would it?"

After an uncomfortable pause, I added, "Don't worry, Steve. It's all way behind me now. The Duke's been good to you, and I probably deserved what I got—for blind stupidity if not for what I was actually accused of. Anyway, that's not why I'm here."

After a long exhale, Steve said, "I'm glad to hear it. And just so you know, I'm going to tell the Duke about this conversation if it seems to go anywhere. Just in case that matters to you."

"It doesn't. As you say, he probably knows all of it anyway."

Just then our waiter appeared, delivering stiff paper menus, two glasses of water, and a brief recitation of the day's specials. The interruption gave me the chance to organize my thoughts now that Steve acknowledged he was a conduit to the Duke. After the waiter departed, I started in.

"When did the Duke ask you to investigate Julio Guzman?"

Steve looked at me quizzically and said, "I really don't remember. It's been months, for sure. Is that what this is about?"

Ignoring the question, I asked, "Did he tell you why he wanted you to investigate Guzman?"

Steve seemed uncomfortable. "Not at first. I thought it was somehow related to a case involving one of Guzman's clinics. Maybe it was, too. He told me later that Guzman was . . . dating . . . your mother."

"This was after it was common knowledge they were getting a divorce?"

"Maybe. I guess it didn't really change what I was doing. The Duke was just looking for information. You know as well as I do how he leverages information."

"Did you independently discover the relationship between my mother and Guzman?"

Steve thought about that before responding, "You know, I never did. It never appeared in anything I saw or heard. Are you saying it never happened?"

"No. I'm sure it happened, but I'm also sure they were discreet. I think Betty told the Duke herself. I think she tried to draw some blood."

The waiter reappeared to take our orders in the ensuing pause. Steve opted for the vegetable lasagna, and I went with the grilled mahi with roasted asparagus. We both ordered unsweetened iced tea. When the waiter left, I started again.

"The Duke said you talked to someone in the DEA and learned about their unproven suspicion that Guzman was still a partner in a cocaine business with two other Colombians. How did you know to even make the call to the DEA? Where did your suspicion come from?"

Steve sighed before saying, "Bank records. Held by his accountants. I'm not going to discuss the 'how' but when I got into it there was too much cash flowing into the business at regular intervals with odd purchases to match it down to the penny. It looked like laundering. So I made some calls."

"Who did you call, Steve?"

"I called a buddy of mine at the FBI and another one at DEA. The FBI had nothing. The DEA had next to nothing. Just smoke with no fire."

"The Duke made it sound like the fire was smoldering a little. Like DEA was looking into it."

"I don't know what to tell you, Jack. I don't know of any investigation."

"So give me your DEA friend's cell phone number. I'd like to ask him about it myself. Just to put an end to the speculation."

Steve gave me his best interrogation room stare and said, "Your mother's dead, Jack. What's the point of digging up dirt now?"

As I was mulling over a response, the waiter delivered our food and drinks. Steam rose from both plates in the crisp, dry air. Picking up my fork, I looked up at Steve and said, "There may be no point. But the Duke thinks my mother's death may not be a suicide. He has his reasons for not involving the police. I want to know if he's completely full of shit. It's that simple, Steve. It's personal for me."

Silently, Steve pulled out his phone, scrolled through his contacts, and arrived at a name and number. He put the phone on the table and said, "I can't help you there, Jack. Now, I've got to use the men's room."

He got up abruptly and went into the building. His phone was faceup, revealing a name and number I quickly memorized. When Steve came back, I said with a smile, "I thought the Duke required you to keep your phone on you at all times during business hours."

Returning the smile, Steve asked, "Did it ring while I was gone?"

"It didn't."

"Then what's the harm?"

CHAPTER SIXTEEN

Back in my room after a pleasant walk back to Rockerman Road, I stretched out on the bed with the intention of taking a nap. Sleep wouldn't come as competing thoughts fought for attention in my conscious mind. Bobby's death had clearly haunted my mother, and the Duke had very purposefully absented himself from any emotional support. The Duke apparently placed no weight on the cumulative effect of prolonged grief as an explanation for Betty's death. My own thoughts drifted to the Duke's report that Betty had not been drinking for several months and to the loose ends in her apartment—the unwashed dishes, the wineglass, the unmade bed, the unfinished portrait. There was no tangible connection to Julio Guzman, and I couldn't assign a legitimate motive for murder to him based on what I knew. Or, more accurately, what I didn't know. I needed information.

My intention had been to call the DEA agent after I got the suicide note from Lauren, but the afternoon was wasting away, and I decided it was unlikely anything in the note would significantly affect my questioning anyway. Reaching down, I pulled my cell phone from the pocket of my jeans and punched in the number I had seen on Steve's phone. Staring at the ceiling while the phone rang, I guessed that the agent wouldn't answer an unrecognized number. I was wrong. Startling me, a male voice answered, "You must be Jack Girard." When I failed to respond immediately, the man chuckled and continued, "Don't freak out, Jack. Steve Amos let me know you would be calling."

Finally able to speak after sitting up and swinging my feet off the bed, I replied, "Okay, then. For a second, I was thinking DEA surveillance was better than advertised. I guess you're Pablo Mercado."

"Yes, I am, Jack. And I'd really like to help you, if I can. You don't know it, but we have an odd connection. My youngest brother was a defensive end at Palmetto when you were a senior at Coral Gables. I was in the stands, on leave from the Army, when you threw for 250 yards and ran for another hundred and a couple of touchdowns. My brother said he never even touched you the entire game. He was so pissed, he wanted to grab you by that long blond hair you had sticking out of your helmet. I had to laugh. When Amos mentioned your name it came back to me, and I wondered why I never heard of your college career."

This wasn't how I expected the call to start, but I replied, "Well, the big schools weren't too interested in me as a quarterback, so I went to UF with my brother and did the track and field thing. Unless you were a track nerd, you wouldn't have heard of either one of us."

The chatty agent followed with, "I guess that explains it, but you looked like a big-timer to me. It's hard to understand what these recruiters are looking for half the time. Anyway, I understand you're looking for information on Julio Guzman. Let me start by telling you I have very little concrete intel. There is an ongoing investigation that sort of backed into Guzman, and your buddy Steve Amos tipped us to several financial transactions that raised some eyebrows. But nothing formal is going on there. Yet.

This might eventually turn into something for the FBI. So what do you want to know?"

I took a moment to gather my thoughts and then led with, "Pablo, my understanding is that Guzman is a one-third partner in a cocaine wholesaling operation based in Colombia that uses Guzman's Miami healthcare system to launder cash. Is that accurate?"

"I think that's accurate as far as it goes. We can't prove any of it at the moment and we are only just now getting a grip on the size of the drug business. These guys were smart. It's a small, tight group of childhood friends who managed to keep their ambitions in check as the money started growing. There's very little turnover in the organization, which is why they've stayed under the radar. The transactions are relatively small. There are no former members to talk to or turn. It's impossible to get an informant inside. It's as if these guys have no succession plan. Like they intend to run it out themselves and then retire. It's smart business from the standpoint of security, but it means they have to keep getting their hands dirty to run it. They don't trust anyone who hasn't been along for the whole ride."

This outpouring from the garrulous DEA man tickled my memory of something the Duke had said while I was doing some serious drinking. Trying to put my finger on it, I said, "I think I'm interested in the dirty hands part. Pablo, given the tight security, if Guzman or even one of the other two partners found out about a leak or discovered that someone close to them was a possible leak, how would they handle it?"

"Well, I don't know for certain, but based on my experience with groups like this, they would handle it decisively and violently. Not just to plug the leak but also as a reminder to the others in the group."

"What if it was someone not exactly in the group but maybe a wife or girlfriend?"

Mercado thought about that for a few seconds and then offered, "I think then you might get more of a finesse play. I could see one of the big three choosing to deal with it on his own to avoid involving the other two. The last thing they want is for the other partners to lose trust. Trust is the only thing—not the money, not the guns—that keeps a group like this together. When that's gone, it's all gone."

I mulled that over. As I did, I felt the phone vibrate, letting me know a text had arrived. Pushing forward, I got to the heart of it. "Pablo, based on what you know, is Julio Guzman capable of killing someone he views as a security risk?"

"Ha ha. That's an easy one, Jack. He absolutely is and I wouldn't be surprised if he already has. These guys have been doing this quietly for almost twenty years. It's hard to imagine there's never been a threat in all that time. And Guzman has the most to lose since he's also the head of a high profile legitimate business here. At least it's outwardly legitimate. I'd bet Guzman's take from the healthcare network dwarfs his take on the drug side at this point. Healthcare is a high profit business these days. He doesn't want anything screwing that up".

The Duke's theory, much as I had discounted it, began to sound more plausible. Realistic, even.

"Well, I guess that's about all I need, Pablo. Thanks. You have a perspective I was missing."

"No problem, Jack. Just remember I've given you very few actual facts. I hope you're not planning to do anything with them yourself. If this leads you anywhere, call me back. We can actually use the help in these budget-cutting times."

And with that he was gone, leaving me sitting on the bed, staring vacantly out the window, unsure what to do next. I had the impression Mercado wanted me to do some investigating, but how would I know when to stop? I had no idea where the trip wires were. Plus, I wasn't really interested in the drug business per se. I was just trying to come to a conclusion about motive. Did I really need to know more than I did right then? Kicking that around in my head, I suddenly remembered the text. Fumbling my way to the text screen on my phone, I saw that it was from Lauren. Opening it, I felt a rush of anticipation. There was a photo with text underneath: "I hope this brings you some peace, Jack. The pen is in the evidence bag."

Wait. What pen? I looked at the photo. It showed a spiral-ring artist's sketch pad open to a page of stiff white paper with hand-writing on it. My mother's handwriting. In red ink. This was not what I expected, but I didn't stop to think about it. I read the note, enlarging it with my thumb and forefinger.

This is not the end I would have planned for myself, even 10 years ago in the darkest days of my life. But now, with the light shining brighter than it ever has, I see clearly the consequences of the choices I've made, choices I'd make again even knowing the result. I hope with all my heart this is not an ending, but the beginning of a new journey where my love will find you again. Never doubt my love, Jack.

There was no salutation or signature. I sat staring at the screen, reading my mother's words over and over, imagining her soft-edged voice reciting them aloud, until I finally dropped the phone on the floor and held my head in my hands, elbows on my knees, letting another wave of anguish wash over me.

I didn't cry. After a time, I sat up and unwittingly experienced the revelation that had eluded me. My mother had indeed taken her own life, but she had done it under pressure. Bobby's bottle of ink, sitting on the table next to where she was found, was not just a clue but a message—to me personally. I had expected the note to be written on Bobby's creamy yellow stationery with his elegant Mont Blanc pen in the deep blue ink he treasured. I had seen the paper, the pen, and the ink bottle and thought instinctively she had used them to write the note in tribute to her son. But if she had, I now realized, the police would have taken all three as a matter of routine. But they were in her room. Instead, she used an ordinary sketchbook and an inexpensive artist's pen, the likes of which I had seen her use many times. The pens came in 24-packs of assorted colors and she had chosen red, the color of warning. The cut-glass bottle of ink sitting on the table, appearing to be just another bottle of perfume to a casual observer, was the clear signal she had deliberately taken it from the drawer with Bobby's picture and placed it where she knew I would recognize it for what it was. Reading her words again, I wondered how many times she had considered using that ink to draft similar words through the years, as she watched her own eyes shifting uneasily under the baleful scrutiny she found in the tabletop mirror.

I could feel her resolve to set things right this time. Thinking about it, I realized that Julio Guzman wouldn't have known anything about Bobby's note or ever guessed at the significance of the ink bottle. I was beginning to circle around a conclusion. But then I remembered that the Duke had never read Bobby's note before I forced it on him in the condominium. He didn't know about the ink bottle either, at least before Betty died.

CHAPTER SEVENTEEN

I spent the remainder of the afternoon and evening preparing words of my own for the memorial service in the morning. I stopped thinking about how my mother died and remembered why she lived. I drifted past the rocky shoals on the stream of her life and noted instead the vibrant colors and depth. She had been by turns impulsive, free-spirited, adventurous, charismatic, curious, determined, defeated, and resolved. I wished I had been a better son, recognizing only then the qualities in her that gave me hope for my own redemption. When I was done, interrupted only by a dinner tray Marta tactfully left at the door, I lay in bed, peacefully contemplating the days to come before lapsing into the deepest sleep I had experienced in many months.

The service itself was as the Duke anticipated. The picturesque Plymouth Congregational Church, built of stone in the Spanish mission style on the southern edge of Coconut Grove during the early 1900s, was sadly quiet. The Donovan family was absent, as were the employees of Duke Girard & Associates, presumably at the request of the Duke himself. He dared not let those he commanded observe him in his weakest moment. Instead, the charming, narrow nave of the church contained a small group of men and women I didn't recognize, mostly friends of Betty she had accumulated in the last few years. It struck me how much of her life had been devoted to the Duke, Bobby, and me. I hoped with my brief speech to give these strangers a broader perspective on the strength of her attachments and the selflessness that had been theirs to claim. Judging by the kind words I heard as they exited the chapel, I succeeded in this.

The Duke, for his part, gave a touching but passionate speech focusing on the earliest days of their marriage and the care Betty provided when he returned from war, scarred and emotionally damaged.

"Thank you all for taking this time from your busy lives to share this memorial to a singular life. Looking out, I see recognition in your eyes, probably the result of seeing my commercials on TV. But, of course, you don't know me. You simply have a sense of me. Betty Donovan knew me. She had that rare ability to make anyone she encountered feel significant, important even. Your thoughts mattered to her. She took the time to actually hear you. I know you've felt this yourselves. A smile from her felt like a reward. But with me, it was a little different. Betty literally saved my life."

The audience shifted audibly as the Duke's voice softened after a pause.

"When I came back from the war, I was in real trouble. I had been wounded, of course, but that was nothing. Thousands of soldiers had it worse than me. My trouble was that I had become unmoored from ordinary feelings of humanity and couldn't see any way to reattach. Things I'd seen—and done—created a barrier that was insurmountable. So I was perfectly indifferent to what future, if there was one, I would experience from that point on. But Betty loved me, without reservation. And she refused to accept my indifference when it would have been easy to let me drift away. It was the power of her life-force, her fundamental decency, her passion for living that slowly led me back to my family, my two beautiful boys, and the future that was far more rewarding than I deserved."

He went on to express gratitude for kindnesses I didn't remember in this confessional tone I had never heard. I was moved, and told him as much afterward, as we descended the front steps of the church together. Stopping at the bottom, turning and holding my shoulders in both hands, the Duke gave me the hard black stare I had come to recognize when something important was coming.

"Jack, the bond between your mother and me was unbreakable. The divorce—nothing!—would ever change that. Have you ever experienced a thing like that?"

The question caught me off guard and I mumbled my reply: "I think I might have. Once."

"There's no *might*, Son. This is something you *know*. It changes you."

He turned and walked to the adjacent parking lot alone, leaving me standing there, mentally treading water in a deep pool of memory where my feet could not quite touch the bottom.

So it was no surprise that I wasn't paying close attention as I meandered along the path to the lot where I had left the Jeep, tucked away off of Devon Road in a tree-shrouded circular configuration. The Jeep was ahead, the only vehicle in sight, the other mourners long gone. The sun was high in the sky, casting everything below it in a crisp, clear light, marked off by sharply drawn shadows among the surrounding trees. As I approached the Jeep, I was vaguely aware of the smooth rumble of a finely tuned engine entering the lot from the road behind me and to the left. Thinking nothing of it but subconsciously assessing my surroundings, I was ten feet from the Jeep when I heard car doors opening and the heavy tread of two men exiting the vehicle now thirty feet behind me. I slowed my pace but still didn't turn, unsure of whether these two posed any threat to me. They did.

"Jack Girard," a Hispanic-accented voice announced, pronouncing the "i" like an "e." "My employer would like a word with you."

Turning now, I saw the speaker standing outside the driver's door of a large black Mercedes-Benz sedan. He was tall, maybe 6'1", and appeared to be in good shape, although it was hard to know with certainty because he was wearing a loose-fitting navy-blue suit with the coat buttoned at the waist. He was approximately forty years old with thick black hair pulled back from his tanned angular face and held behind his head by a metallic clip. He held his hands loosely at his sides and maintained a shoulder-width stance with his feet. A potential fighting stance, with the possibility of a weapon hidden by that buttoned jacket. In my mind I heard Mr. An instructing me, "You must close the distance to this possible adversary." I slowly stepped toward the man, conveying as best I could confusion tinged with fear.

"Who are you? I don't understand."

As I eased forward, I saw the second man standing outside the passenger door, left hand on the roof of the car with the right hidden from view. He was also wearing a blue suit, covering a substantially bulkier frame than that of the driver, who responded, "Don't worry. My employer just wants to talk to you. About your mother."

I was now five feet away, keeping the driver between me and the second man, who could not see all of me and made no move to change his position—a tactical error. Still outwardly expressing confusion—"Well, who's your employer? I'm not following—" I edged my left foot forward to achieve blow-striking balance. The man before me was no longer thinking of me as a serious threat, if he ever did, and reached out as he stepped toward me as if to seize my arm, a smile spreading across his face as he said, "Take it easy. This won't take long."

I suddenly punched him hard in his exposed sternum with my closed right fist. I heard the hollow crack of a fractured rib just before the expulsion of air and the shocked cry of pain. If the blow had been clean, it might have stopped his heart, but it wasn't (I was still wearing a suit). I pressed forward before he could recover and delivered a straight-legged kick to the groin that crumpled him at my feet. Which is when I heard the unmistakable click of the safety being taken off of a handgun. I looked up to find the second man leveling a snub-nosed pistol at my head, using the roof of the car to steady the shot. I considered diving under the car and attempting to kick his feet out from under him but, in a split-second calculation, I realized the distance was too great and the space too compressed to generate enough power to knock over this two-hundred-plus-pound man, even if he didn't move. I was beaten.

Looking more carefully at the second man, I noticed he was heavyset, at least fifty years old, with a close-cropped, military cut to his silvery hair. His round white face housed a bulbous nose interspersed with the tiny telltale red blood vessels of the heavy drinker. His puffy blue eyes were emotionless and his thin-lipped slash of a mouth was shut tight. Only the heavy raised eyebrows betrayed a hint of surprise. I was thinking about how I could get to the other side of the car as I said, "Don't shoot. You got me."

Which is when the rear driver's-side door opened wide, apparently pushed from within. The man with the gun said, in American-accented English, "Get in." The man at my feet was now struggling to stand, using the car's frame to push himself up as he grimaced in pain. The sleeve of his suit was torn and he was sweating profusely. He was pissed. I noticed now that the second man didn't have his finger on the trigger of the gun; apparently, shooting me in broad daylight was not a real option. I thought about turning and running for the Jeep, but that would only trade one problem for another because the Mercedes blocked the parking lot exit. I was sure I could run past the car and make it down Devon to the more heavily traveled Main Highway, but then what? Flag down a passing vehicle? Plus, I was curious about who was in the car. My decision made, I stepped toward the open rear door and ducked in quickly, before the angry driver had time to renew his attack, which he so plainly planned to do as he edged past the open front door in an attempt to flank me. Smiling at him, I closed the door and turned to see the bemused face I presumed belonged to Julio Guzman.

"You are indeed Betty's son. There is spirit in you."

He was not what I expected, and I realized I had never seen a picture of him in the various news accounts of his business dealings I had encountered over the years. He sat slightly askew in the spacious rear compartment of the car, wearing jeans, well-worked cowboy boots, and a faded, red, raw silk long-sleeved shirt with the sleeves rolled up to mid-forearm. He was slender of frame but conveyed the impression of coiled strength. His face bore lines at the corners of the eyes and mouth, attesting to long exposure to sun and weather, but his immaculate white teeth, revealed in an easy smile, reflected some level of vanity, as yet unrevealed. His shaggy blond hair framed his face with youthful insouciance and his alert brown eyes conveyed intelligence as they scanned me quickly before settling on mine. On balance, he looked more like a retired surfer or rock musician

than a businessman or narcotics mogul. I would pin his age at
fifty-six or fifty-seven.

In the enveloping silence, I was aware of my own breathing.
Slow and steady; I was surprisingly calm. Choosing not to address
the reference to my mother, I said, "Your employee said you would
like to have a word with me. What might that be?"

Guzman paused a moment to consider his response, clasping
his hands together in his lap.

"Jack," he began with only the faintest hint of an accent, "you
have been asking questions about me and my business. First your
father and now you."

My face must have revealed the surprise I felt because he continued, "It should not be a shock that my sources of information
within the law enforcement community are extensive. The next
secret the DEA keeps will be the first."

He laughed derisively.

"The FBI and the local police are not much better. Corruption
is so much easier now that everything is political. Everyone has an
angle to play or an enemy to take down, so the information floats
about freely. You don't even have to pay for it."

"Most of the time," he added with a chuckle. "I understood
your father's motivation at the start, and I exercised patience
because no harm was done. But now that your mother has
passed, I learn that more questions are being asked. I have to ask
myself why. What is the motivation now? Is the son serving the
interests of the father? Is this about spite? Or vengeance? These
are important questions, Jack, because I must understand your
resolve. And your father's. The FBI is now poking around in my
affairs, and I intend to deal with that very soon. I must know
if my problem is as I imagine it or if it is something different.

Something personal. So tell me, Jack, why are you interested in me?"

His smile remained.

As he was talking, it occurred to me that I could kill him right then if I had a mind to. Those clasped hands could not unfold soon enough to stop me from delivering a hard strike to his exposed trachea, leading to an agonizing—and silent—asphyxiation, which might even give me a fighter's chance of escaping the vehicle and getting a reasonable head start before the two henchmen knew what had happened. But this was a fantasy. At best, I would be on trial for murder, and at worst, I would be dead with a bullet in my back. I didn't like either option, particularly because I wasn't sure this man was my enemy. It seemed that he knew all the facts but was unsure about motive. Just like me. I decided to see if we could gain clarity together. After that, I would formulate an exit plan on the fly.

I began, "Well, Mr. Guzman, I don't know exactly what the Duke's motives are now. I know what mine are. It's pretty simple, really. I want to know why my mother died."

There was something there in his eyes. Surprise? Alarm? He unclasped his hands and clenched his right fist. No longer bemused, he asked in a low, calm voice that unsettled me, "How does this involve me, Jack?"

"Well, my father told me about your . . . relationship . . . with my mother. He . . . suggested . . . that she might have been trying to . . . leverage some knowledge of your business activities into a . . . different relationship than the one you had. It occurred to me that this might have happened at a bad time for you. As you say, the FBI was starting to look around. This might have caused you to take a very . . . aggressive step. Depending on how you perceived the threat."

I stopped there and watched Guzman process a number of thoughts as he clenched and unclenched his fist, eyes staring blankly forward through the windshield. Finally turning to face me, he said, "So it is vengeance. Your father has enticed you with the idea that your mother's death was more than just a suicide. You have clumsily explored the idea and now you are here, seeking certainty."

He paused for a moment, studying me, as if to discern my commitment to the truth. Or my gullibility. I held his eyes steadily, waiting.

"I am going to tell you something I'm now sure your father did not, Jack. I mean no disrespect to your mother, but this thing was hers to tell you and now she cannot, leaving it to me, it seems. I will not discuss my relationship with Betty but I will tell you, and I don't mind telling you, that she touched me very deeply. She— what is the word?—extracted emotions from me I thought were buried long ago, never to be uncovered. This was a gift. For which I am grateful."

His voice lowered to a near whisper as he looked down at his hands resting on his lap. "I would not harm the bearer of such a gift."

I was softening. I was very familiar with the gift he described, having rejected it myself many times. But then Guzman delivered the heavy blow.

"You see, Jack, it was your mother who ended our relationship months ago. She always knew how it was with me and was content to experience our pleasures as they came. To savor them. But then she met someone else. It was love, the real thing, and she wanted to tell me herself before she was forced to deceive me. I respected that. Her name was Gina Martelli. She was a real estate broker in New York City."

He stopped to gauge my reaction. Which was pure shock. My mother's new love was a woman. Thoughts swarmed through my head like bees. How could I not have seen this part of my own mother? I envisioned her slide into drugs and alcohol after Bobby's death in a new way. Did she regret not revealing this part of herself to her troubled son? Did she bear the full weight of his death alone? Wait a minute. Did he just say "was"?

"Mr. Guzman, this is a lot to take in," I managed to say. "But where is Gina Martelli now? She must be devastated."

"I thought of this myself when I first learned about your mother, Jack. I didn't know if anyone even knew how to contact her. So I tried to reach her myself. It was the least I could do."

He hesitated.

"But then I learned that Gina Martelli has not been seen for more than a week. I think your friend Lauren Kaplan could confirm that there is a missing persons report on file in Manhattan. Ms. Martelli's car was found in a parking garage at LaGuardia. There was no sign of foul play, but she was not booked on any flight. As of now, no one knows what happened to her."

Still processing the implications, I asked, "Did my father know about my mother and . . . Gina?"

"I believe he did. She said she was going to tell him right after she told me."

I thought about that. Was this another example of the Duke's selective reality? Had he erased this repulsive and inconvenient fact from his life? Or was there something else that caused him to skip over that part of my mother's story as he related it to me? Is it possible Betty hesitated to tell the Duke about her relationship with Gina while the divorce was pending? All good questions; Guzman didn't know the answer to any of them.

It was time to go.

"Mr. Guzman, I appreciate your telling me this."

Swallowing hard, I reached for the door handle as if to leave. Guzman seized my left wrist with a surprisingly strong grip. I resisted the impulse to dislocate his elbow, which presented itself as an easy target. I sensed that he meant no immediate harm.

He said, "Jack, let me be clear. I believe you will not concern yourself with me anymore. I would hate to discover I was wrong about this. I came here today because I knew you would be here, but I could have met with you somewhere else. I chose this place because I hoped to feel something—maybe closure—about your mother. I stayed outside, out of respect for you and your father."

After a pause for reflection, he said, "Honestly, I still only feel the loss. The wound is not healing. Will her ashes be interred somewhere?"

I wasn't expecting that question, but I answered without hesitation.

"No. My father and I will be spreading her ashes on the water by Fowey Light at dawn on Saturday. She didn't want a permanent marker, apparently. I think I understand that."

With a slightly distanced look in his eyes, Guzman said, "There are no permanent markers, Jack. They will all be dust one day. Your mother knew where her memory would reside. I wish you calm seas. You may go."

And with that he released me. I opened the door and stepped out into the bright sunlight. The driver glared at me from a standing position near the front fender of the car. The second man was in his same spot, but had lowered his gun. His expression was impassive. With no further word, I turned and started for the Jeep, alert for any movement behind me. Instead, I heard the car doors open and close and the big car roll out of the parking lot onto Devon Road heading east. Alone now, I took off my suit jacket and loosened my tie, aware that I had begun to sweat. I could feel my fingers tingling from the adrenaline crash I knew I was experiencing. Arriving at the Jeep, I threw the jacket on the passenger seat and climbed in.

Sitting there, my thoughts were jumbled. On impulse, I dug my phone out of my pocket and googled Gina Martelli in New York City. Sure enough, a short story in the *New York Post* reported her missing last Monday, having not appeared at her office for two appointments with clients. The police were seeking information after the discovery of her car at the airport. A picture with the story revealed an attractive woman in her mid-forties with short dark hair and dark eyes. A broad smile lit up her slender face with positive energy. She looked like someone who laughed a lot.

As I stared at the picture, I thought of my mother, hoping to feel some sort of connection between the two. There was nothing, but I could envision that face in the unfinished painting in my mother's condo. Which, of course, proved nothing. There was still no direct connection between my mother and Martelli. Could Guzman be lying about all of it? Why would he? On the other hand, might Guzman have felt emotionally betrayed by my mother? He was clearly experiencing strong emotions. But I had to admit he seemed uniquely self-possessed and under control. Not the type to react violently out of jealousy or damage to his ego. But a threat to his business? Definitely.

Considering these things, I realized there was no point in sticking around Miami. The forced meeting with Guzman provided the last of the information I was likely to uncover. I wasn't ready to confront the Duke about gaps in the story he told me and I wanted to think about what Guzman himself most wanted to know: the Duke's motives. Finally, if I spent the night I would be sorely tempted to call Lauren and ask her to meet me for a drink.

But I didn't like the fact that Guzman had mentioned her by name. Until this was finally settled, involving her further could be unhealthy for both of us. Far better that Guzman, assuming he was watching, believed I was done with him. So I started the Jeep and headed directly for home. To Key West.

CHAPTER EIGHTEEN

I pulled into my parking spot behind Jack's Hideaway three and a half hours later, having only stopped for gas and a Diet Pepsi. The trip provided plenty of time to let my thoughts settle, and I began to feel bolts falling into place, like the combination locking mechanism of a safe. I walked through the back door of the bar still wearing my black suit pants, crisply starched white shirt, and silver, pink, and black repp tie. Tracy was behind the bar with her back turned, pulling cans of beer from the cooler at the front. There was a typical Tuesday evening crowd of after-work locals and pre-dinner tourists, buzzing happily about what the day had delivered or what the night had to offer. From the jukebox, the Allman Brothers were hitting their stride on "One Way Out." Pausing to take in the scene, I felt gratitude that this small port in life's storm was mine.

As if sensing me, Tracy turned and looked directly at me, surprise, confusion, and happiness competing for control of her expression. Happiness prevailed, and as I stepped toward her behind the bar, she raced over to hug me, mashing her face hard against my chest. Her wild red hair tickled my chin as her breasts noticeably pressed into my stomach. Pulling herself away, she said,

"We've missed you, Jack. I hope everything turned out okay, but we're glad to have you back."

Who is we? I wondered.

She cast a curious glance at my tie, and I realized she had probably never seen me in a suit. I also remembered that I had never told her exactly why I had left. Not wanting to broach that topic behind the bar with customers waiting, I said, "It went about as well as it could, Tracy. I got a few things done early, so here I am. I guess I should have called, right? Well, let me get out of your way and we'll talk later. And by the way, I have to leave again on Friday, back Saturday or Sunday. Okay?"

Still smiling, Tracy responded, "Whatever you need, Jack. You're the boss."

"Sometimes I wonder," I chuckled as I stepped back into the customer area. Standing near the rear door, I had a good view of the whole crowd. Tracy noticed me looking and shouted, "She's not here! Hasn't been since Sunday!"

I waved sheepishly and turned toward the exit. I'd only had a passing thought of Anna Markova, but Tracy had seen right through me. No one had ever referred to me as transparent, but Tracy always made me feel that way. Was that a good thing? It seemed to work for us in our professional relationship, but I mused about the dynamics of a personal combination like that.

"Jesus, Jack, don't even think about it!"

With every intention of taking my own advice, I crossed the courtyard to my apartment. But I was struck by the fact that I had experienced feelings of attraction toward two different women in the last five days. That hadn't happened in the last two years since it ended with Lauren. Huh. And I'd actually talked to Lauren just yesterday. Was I over her? It didn't really feel that way in Miami.

Opening the apartment door, I stepped inside and looked around. A small kitchen to the left, a combination living room and dining room to the right. Plank wood floors below and rough beamed ceiling above. IKEA furniture throughout. A far cry from the Duke's monument to himself or the Donovans' generational estate. But it felt snug and comfortable to me. I'd become happy here, I realized, or at least as close to happy as I'd been since Bobby died.

Entering the bedroom, I sat heavily on the edge of the bed and allowed my thoughts to drift toward my brother, something I reflexively refused to do for many years for fear of the knifelike pain to follow. I had tortured myself wondering why I never thought about the fact that we didn't talk about girls the way brothers do; why I had dismissed the fact that he never had a girlfriend as long as I knew him. Of course, I didn't either, at least until my junior year of college. With everything I was doing, it didn't seem odd. My relationships were friendly but casual—and I thought Bobby was the same. Girls were certainly attracted to him, I knew. I was angry that he never confided in me and then angry with myself for judging him. It was best to let it be, swallow the pain, and quell the anger. Mr. An had at least given me that meditative skill.

But now I found myself smiling, sifting through the images, and pausing on the fiercely determined look on Bobby's face as he crossed the finish line first at the state championship track meet during our junior year of high school, passing three runners grinding as best they could in the closing fifty meters. It wasn't that he was accelerating past them at the end; it was that he was slowing down less as the tape came into view. He held his speed and refused to buckle. That was exactly what winning looked like: the effort, the exhaustion, the purity of it. Had I ever experienced a moment like that? Some would point to victories of my own through the years, but I wasn't so sure. Did I ever really give everything? Bobby did. And so did Betty.

The thought of my mother led to the nagging sensation that I was missing something. It was all there, I knew. A connection. I could feel my subconscious mind working to pull the right strands of thought together, but they wouldn't come. I knew from experience not to become frustrated, but to let it be. The answer would arrive in its own time.

Suddenly conscious of my surroundings again, I noticed the rumpled bedding behind me. I thought back to Friday night. Or, more accurately, to Saturday morning. And Anna. If I laid my head against the pillow, I was sure the scent of her would greet me.

"Maybe I should change the sheets," I said aloud.

Silently laughing at myself, I did just that, stuffing the used sheets in a hamper in the closet. With that done, I changed clothes, opting for jeans and a long-sleeved Bob Marley tee-shirt. I drifted into the kitchen and microwaved a Lean Cuisine vegetable lasagna. I thought about opening the 2015 Coppola Director's Cut red blend that beckoned from the six-bottle rack I kept on the counter by the refrigerator, but decided against it and unscrewed the top on a bottle of Propel fitness water instead. Small steps toward clarity of mind and purpose. I sat at the dining table and ate in silence, waiting for the answer to arrive. It didn't.

With nothing else to do, I wandered back over to the bar and seated myself at a high-top table near the jukebox in the rear. The weeknight crowd was thinning and the second bartender, Jasmine, was behind the bar chatting with a group of three male tourists. Tracy, who had seen me come in, approached the table with what I recognized to be a printout from our accounting software. I held up my hand and said, "No business tonight,

Tracy. We can talk numbers in the morning. I just want to decompress a little."

"Sure, Jack, no problem. But just so you know, we're having a really good month. Reggae Sunday was our best yet and hiring Jasmine away from Schooner Wharf has already paid off. She's got a pretty good local following, and she has a way of getting the tourists to order round two."

In the Key West bar business, getting the tourists to commit to a second round of drinks is significant. Many choose to stop and pop, moving from one bar to the next in an effort to cover all of Old Town in one or two nights. Getting them to abandon that plan and order a second drink was a skill that certain bartenders refined effortlessly. Jasmine, who I had hired a couple of months previously, had the knack. She was a local, having grown up in Bahama Village and graduated from Key West High, and had a natural way of making people comfortable. It didn't hurt that she was a knockout, either. When I was watching, I noticed that she had the ability to pour drinks while maintaining eye contact with her customers, laughing appropriately at their bad jokes and pretending not to notice their furtive glances at her ample cleavage.

"Yep. That was a great hire."

Pausing for a moment, I thought about it and said, "Have a seat, Tracy. Jasmine's got it under control."

As she reached to pull out a chair, she hesitated and looked at me intently, searching my face for clues of meaning. I didn't realize it in the moment, but I think she saw vulnerability there.

"Are you okay, Jack? Can I get you a drink?"

I was a little put off by the questions, sensitive to her innate ability to read me, and worried that I had damaged our relationship by thinking of her beyond the context of the bar.

"I'm fine, Tracy, and no, I don't need a drink. I was just asking you to sit and talk a bit. No big deal."

That might have come out more tersely than I intended. Tracy took her hand off the chair back and said, "I know. No biggie. But I really should get back and start the close-out. Jasmine is due to leave soon. Just let me know if you need something."

Her eyes held mine for an extra second and I could see her mind working hard. Was that indecision? Fear? As she turned and began walking back to the bar, I was surprised to catch myself noticing how great she looked in those tight jeans. Things had definitely changed, but I wasn't sure if that was for the better. I wondered if Tracy had harbored her own imaginings about me and was suddenly unsure about how to handle the prospect of those thoughts becoming real. Or maybe the timing was a problem for her. She knew I had experienced some sort of emotional trauma but didn't know exactly what it was. Maybe she didn't want to be just a shoulder to cry on. I thought of her strong reaction to my interplay with Anna Markova a few nights back. Was that jealousy rather than disdain for Anna's line of work? And what about Anna? Why was she so anxious to see me again?

Admonishing myself, I thought, *Get over yourself, Jack. Just play the cards you see. Both of these women will reveal themselves sooner or later.*

And that's when it hit me. When I drew the connection that had been teasing me. It was the thought of two people, somehow linked. I actually stood up at the table in shock at the clarity of the revelation. It felt like I was in the courtroom during the closing argument in my last trial where I told the jury, "There's an old saying: It's easy to know the truth, but, oh, how difficult to follow it! You know the truth! Your job now is to follow that truth wherever it leads and not be distracted!" Like those jurors, I now knew the truth. The actual truth. It was in my mother's suicide note. At the time I first read it, my state of mind—and possibly my ego—had prevented me from seeing it. Yanking my phone from my back pocket, I pulled up Lauren's text from the day before and scrolled through the note to the last two lines:

I hope with all my heart this is not an ending, but the beginning of a new journey where my love will find you again. Never doubt my love, Jack.

When I first read the note, I assumed both sentences were directed at me, her remaining son. But the first sentence was not to me; it was to Gina Martelli. There was passion and depth there I hadn't noticed before, a sincere wish that a nascent love would not be forever lost. The second sentence included my name to assure Gina that it wasn't meant for her, that she had no concern that Gina doubted her feelings. I knew she had those concerns about me and with good reason, given the distance between us these last years. So Betty provided comfort and assurance to the last two loves of her life while confronting her own imminent death. What an extraordinary woman. It was inexplicably sad that Gina would never receive that comfort unless my mother's heartfelt hope was somehow realized. I didn't know if such things were possible, but I knew with certainty that the man who caused this pain would pay a price for it. There would be justice.

CHAPTER NINETEEN

Wednesday arrived peacefully. Before going to bed Tuesday night, I had thought through where things stood and what my options were. I considered enlisting Lauren to contact the New York police detectives to inquire about the status of the investigation into Gina Martelli's disappearance. I was also interested in knowing if there was any information connecting Martelli to my mother. But as I thought about it, I realized I didn't need more information. What I needed was to confront the Duke. Everything else would flow from that, and I could envision several possible outcomes. Because of the impending hearing at the Monroe County Courthouse on Thursday, there would be no realistic chance to talk to the Duke face-to-face until Friday at the earliest. So when I slipped into bed, I slept soundly, having learned through experience not to live future events before their time. Of course, keeping the past at bay was a harder task, but I was getting better at it with practice. Which led to the first pleasant dream I'd had in years.

I was seated near the bow of a thirty-foot sailboat making way across the foamy turquoise water of Biscayne Bay. It was a warm day and the sun felt good against my skin. I could hear the luffing of the mainsail as the boat began a turn into the wind. Looking back at the cockpit, I saw my mother, smiling radiantly, gently taking over the helm from a seemingly flustered woman I recognized as Gina Martelli. There was no surprise; I seemed to know her. As my mother steered the boat onto a more leeward tack, the sail filled, and the boat surged forward with graceful power. Gina looked at my mother with unabashed affection as she slid her arm around her waist. As my mother tried to explain the basic dynamics of steering a sailboat, Gina burst out laughing, seemingly resigned to her role as the crew and never the captain. Her laugh was infectious, and soon we were all howling. After I woke up and recalled the dream, I realized I couldn't remember the last time I had laughed unreservedly.

So, feeling refreshed, I spent the day catching up on bar business, running errands, and—most importantly—working out. I spent thirty minutes punishing the heavy bag at BodyZone Fitness and another two hours lifting weights. I topped it off by jamming my aging Starboard paddle board in the back of the Jeep and driving the twenty-five miles to the Ramrod Swimming Hole. The wind was surprisingly light for January and the temperature was hovering around eighty-two, so I had a great opportunity to get on the water and tap into the last bit of energy left in me. When I arrived around three the tide was high, and water lapped up to the edges of the fifty-yard channel cut into the coral rock shoreline before unrestrained development was halted in the Lower Keys in 1972. Now, the so-called "swimming hole," a couple of winding miles off the Overseas Highway on Ramrod Key, was a gathering place for locals to bring their dogs or their children to swim in the calm, crystal clear water in the mangrove-lined twenty-foot-wide cut. Tourists had recently found it, much to the grumbling dismay of the residents.

On this day, there were two groups on opposite sides of the channel when I arrived. One group of six twenty-somethings assembled in beach chairs sat along the edge of the cut, beers in hand and loud hip-hop music throbbing from the open trunk of a car backed up behind them. An older group of four on the opposite side was packing up to leave in their Nissan minivan, all the while casting nasty, furtive looks at the festive party across the water. This was a perfect example of the now-frequent problem at the swimming hole: the inability to accommodate the differing views on what a pleasant day near the water entails in a relatively small and remote area. There are no lifeguards or police standing by to mediate. Locals usually try to work things out, while hard-partying tourists tend to do their own thing without much concern for anyone not in their group. Here, I was guessing the hip-hoppers were from somewhere else.

None of this concerned me as I pulled out my board and paddle and dropped in at the head of the cut. After seven or eight strong pulls against a mild current, I was out on the edge of Niles Channel heading west into the setting sun. The subtle strain in my back muscles felt good, and the seventy-three-degree water flowing over my bare feet was invigorating. I was at peace, warm sun on my face, thinking of nothing in particular for the first time in days. Of course, that couldn't last. My subconscious mind was still working and my recent willingness to loosen the reins that had checked it for so long would bring to the surface the dark with the light—in this case a memory I had carefully buried years before.

. . .

I was driving north on Bayshore Drive heading toward Rockerman Road in the two-seat BMW roadster leased for me through
Duke Girard & Associates. It had been five days since my final
meeting with the Duke in his office, and I hadn't spoken to him
since. I also hadn't spoken to my mother, which was the impe-
tus for this trip. It was three o'clock on a Wednesday, and I was
sure she would be home alone. Pulling into the driveway, I felt my
stomach tighten as it did before courtroom appearances when I
was unsure of the outcome. I bypassed the front door and a possible encounter with Marta and walked along the side of the house
toward the rear terrace by the dock. As I reached the back corner
of the house and the full terrace came into view, I saw my mother
seated at the circular glass-topped table we used for barbecues and
casual gatherings by the pool when we were a family. The umbrella
rising from the center of the table was open and Betty's shaded
face was directed toward the canal and tree-filled Kennedy Park.
She was wearing an emerald green sundress, her blond hair falling
loosely on her bare shoulders. A tall glass filled with ice and a clear
liquid I knew to be vodka sat on the table close to the long fingers
of her slender hand. Her index finger tapped the table irregularly.
As I approached, I cleared my throat.

"Hello, Mother."

She slowly turned her head to appraise me, her normally bright
blue eyes dimmed by the shade and slightly unfocused by alcohol.

"My son. My dearest only son. I wondered whether you were
going to do this by phone. This is better."

So she knew.

"I intended to come sooner, but I kept getting tripped up by
my own feelings. I was ashamed, I guess. Sad. I wasn't sure how to
tell you, and then I realized the Duke probably did. I finally just
decided to come see you. No script."

I was standing in the sun, squinting slightly and beginning to perspire. My mother gave no notice of my discomfort and turned to look out at the water again. I dared not pull out a chair to sit in the shade of the umbrella.

"Have you told my parents?"

"No."

I had been avoiding my grandparents, who were probably wondering why I had been hanging around the garage apartment the last few days.

"I have to tell you, Jack, this one took me by surprise. And I'm pretty hard to surprise these days. There are so many things—so many things!—you're capable of. But I never thought cheating was one of them."

She reached for her glass and took a long swallow before continuing.

"I've tried to sort it out and I just can't see it. This isn't you."

She turned again to look at me and held my eyes for several long moments.

"There has to be more to it, Jack. There has to be a reason you would take such a risk. Your father says it's not uncommon for junior associates to pad their billable hours to look more productive to the partners, but that doesn't make sense to me. Your father is the only partner. Why would you lie to him? He didn't have an answer for that and really didn't want to talk about it anymore. It was like he was embarrassed."

After a pause, in a near whisper, "I'm asking you, Jack. What am I missing?"

Here was my chance, forever lost, to square things with my mother. I can't fully explain why I didn't do it, why I couldn't expose the Duke. It would have destroyed their marriage, certainly, and it wouldn't bring Bobby back. But there was something else that held my tongue. Loyalty? Shame? Or fear?

"You're not missing anything, Mom. It's all on me."

She stared at me blankly.

"And I should tell you I'm leaving for a while. I'm going down to Key West to sort things out. Figure things out, more likely. I don't know when I'm coming back. I'm going to leave my car in the driveway for the Duke and I'll take a cab back to Old Cutler. My Jeep is there."

My mother's eyes began to well up, although no tears fell.

"You're not being straight with me, Jack. I know it."

She looked back out at the water.

"You know, it's not shame I'm feeling. I'm not ashamed of you, Jack. I'm disappointed. That's what it is. You've disappointed me."

There was nothing left to say except, "I'm sorry," as I turned to walk away.

. . .

Once again focused on the water before me, I noticed that I was paddling furiously, breathing heavily and drenched in sweat, well over a mile from my launch point. The good with the bad, right? I stopped paddling and sat down on my board, allowing it to drift with the current. I watched the sun moving closer to the western horizon and breathed deeply. A realization came to me as I wondered why that memory had chosen to revisit me today. My mother had been undeniably happier over the last year and now I knew exactly why. She had found her identity, her true self, and was comfortable with the discovery and the love that came with it. She had definitely been more cheerful in our last conversations, however brief they were. I think a part of that cheerfulness was her coming to understand that I—like her—had found my identity after leaving Miami. I think she was happy for me, although she never said it, and even though she never fully understood what drove me away in the first place. I really believe that.

Two hours later, exhausted and hungry, I was at the Looe Key Tiki Bar back on Ramrod Key polishing off a perfectly grilled slab of mahi-mahi. I was drinking water, which mildly irritated the bartender, who could usually count on a good tip when customers ate and drank at the bar. She needn't have worried; I always tipped big out of respect for the profession.

. . .

After settling the bill and earning a bright smile from the bartender, I rolled back to Key West feeling relaxed and settled. My mother's death was still with me, and there was no hiding from the reality we experienced, but I was slowly developing a respectful appreciation for her spiritual facility that comforted me. She was an emotional savant, always able to give exactly what was necessary to those needing solace, even when they couldn't recognize their own pain. I believed this was why Bobby's death haunted her; if he hadn't been away at school, she could have saved him. So she thought. To me, she gave what she could in the following years, but I wasn't receiving, having chosen the typical Girard path of emotional suppression and ambitious striving. I now knew that the Duke had actually done me a favor by knocking me off that path, allowing me to blindly tumble down to Key West where so much more of myself was revealed. I was emerging, as if from hibernation, and it felt good. This was Betty's parting gift, rubbing the sleep from my eyes, like she did when I was a boy.

Back at Jack's Hideaway after a hot shower, I was encouraged, at least, that Tracy was treating me as she always had, which is to say with mock intolerance when I actually tried to take a shift at the bar and make drinks.

"Jesus, Jack! Why don't you go sit over there with the customers and drink the liquor rather than stand back here spilling it! At least you'll get something out of it."

My bartender skills were better than inept, but this sort of comment signaled things were okay with us. I wasn't sure that's where I wanted to leave them, but I certainly wasn't going to push it. All of these thoughts and feelings were new to me and I believed time was on my side.

So the evening played out uneventfully, the only excitement being a commotion out on the street when rival groups of Alabama and Clemson fans drunkenly squared off before realizing that no one was willing to actually throw a punch. So they all pretended to be friends and came into the bar for a round of shots. Easy money. I sent Tracy and Jasmine home early and closed the bar myself, enjoying the physical toil of washing the glasses, cleaning the bar top, and mopping the floor. By the time I got to bed it was past two a.m., and I dropped like a stone, exhausted by the day but satisfied.

CHAPTER TWENTY

U p early the next day, I went for a run around the circumference of Key West covering a little more than ten miles. My timing allowed me to witness a pristine sunrise along Smathers Beach in the company of a scattering of tourists, some having risen early to enjoy the daily ritual and others heading back to their rooms late, marveling that they had seen the sun fall into the sea and rise again in the last twelve hours. As a new resident, I had resisted becoming complacent about the natural beauty of a Caribbean sunrise and hoped to maintain a fitting reverence for these natural masterworks—always varying to some chromatic degree—that we had the privilege of seeing wrought before our eyes every day.

On this day, some water vapor along the horizon created a soft line of purple and orange light as I came around the southeastern corner of Atlantic Boulevard and made my way north along Smathers Beach. By the time I passed the airport, the familiar orange and yellow disk had emerged from the sea, casting magnificent white and yellow reflections across the water to the sand. Four brown pelicans flying at my approximate pace were silhouetted against the sun as they began their morning search for baitfish near the ocean's surface. Feeling my stride lengthen into a comfortable rhythm, I let my mind wander to the case scheduled for hearing later in the afternoon.

I had learned over the years that repetitive physical exertion often produced a state of mind permitting insight and creativity that were otherwise inaccessible to me. It was natural that my mind circled around and rested upon the hearing scheduled later in the day that formed the legitimate basis for my return to the island. The hearing itself posed no great challenge. The defense lawyer in one of my cases had served a motion to dismiss a complaint I had filed, arguing, essentially, that the factual allegations I had presented did not sufficiently state a claim recognized by the law. That was nonsense. I had very carefully drafted the complaint after a thorough interview of my client, Natalie Prudhomme, a server/bartender at a Key West boutique hotel called the Pirate's Retreat. I believed Natalie's story and thought her case could have some broader local impact. She had recently moved to Key West from Mobile, Alabama, after falling in love with the town while on vacation with a group of college sorority sisters.

She found the job at the Pirate's Retreat through an ad on Craigslist, not realizing at the time that the ad was always running. The hotel itself consisted of two Victorian-era Old Town houses connected by a central garden offering a pool and private hot tub. Each house, shaded by large banyan and royal poinciana trees, had a bar on the first floor leading out to a broad veranda overlooking the garden. Breakfast was provided each morning in a club room facing the street. There were twenty rooms in all and the hotel's website conveyed an aura of mysterious romance catering to adventurous couples and singles.

The problem was the hotel's owner, Miles Highgate Jr., a fifty-year-old New York–based real estate investor who had inherited $150 million and managed to reduce that fortune to about

$80 million during his "career" buying and selling commercial real estate throughout the Northeast. Still, $80 million was a lot of money and Miles spent much of his time trying to convince his friends and acquaintances that he had earned it himself through shrewd market timing. He bought the Pirate's Retreat a few years back for $4.8 million, intending to use it as a periodic getaway for himself and the investment bankers who kept his business afloat. That it could also generate cash flow serving other guests was a secondary benefit; the primary job was to keep the bankers happy. And for that Miles had the boorish idea to staff the hotel almost entirely with young, attractive women recruited through Craigslist and similar sites.

Like Natalie, they were never told how the hotel operated, only that they were expected to be "friendly" to the single guests who arrived. As a result, they were subjected to innuendo, leering, propositions, pats on the ass, and worse until they had had enough and quit, oftentimes taking jobs at other Key West hotels, bars, and restaurants. They didn't complain for fear of being blackballed in the Key West hospitality industry and felt lucky enough just to have gotten out of the Pirate's Retreat and landed on their feet.

Natalie's experience was a little different. Miles himself was on hand when Natalie was interviewed by the manager of the hotel and was impressed by her bartending experience, but was particularly attracted to her exotic appearance, which was three-quarters Choctaw Native American and one-quarter French/European. Tall and lean, with long silky black hair, coppery dark skin, and incongruous blue eyes, she was hired on the spot. Miles insisted on taking her on her first tour of the hotel. He attempted to be charming as he described the layout and the clientele but only succeeded in being creepy when he discussed the tips that could be earned by conveying the right "attitude" to the single male guests.

Having worked in some of Mobile's downtown hot spots, Natalie believed she was up to the task of handling harmlessly aggressive customers. But she wasn't ready for Miles himself.

Within her first two weeks, she noticed Miles watching her as she set up the bars in both locations and interacted with customers. He seemed to appear almost magically when business was slow and took the opportunity to regale her with stories of his business acumen, sucking in his gut and insecurely running his fingers through his receding blond hair. When he persistently asked whether she had a boyfriend or was dating anyone, Natalie politely deflected or changed the subject. Miles was, as a result, getting frustrated. He was planning to go back to New York in a few days and had gotten nowhere in his attempted conquest of his new employee. So, on his second-to-last night, he hung around on the veranda, drinking scotch, making small talk with the guests and watching Natalie through the open French doors as she worked the bar, bending over for ice, reaching for glasses, and smiling—seductively, as Miles viewed it—at the guests seated in front of her in twos and threes. Finally, as the last guests were leaving, Natalie began breaking down the bar and moving the most expensive bottles of liquor into the storeroom at the rear of the house next to the then-empty kitchen. On her second trip, after placing two bottles of premium tequila on a shelf, she turned to find Miles blocking the doorway, his face red, his eyes slightly glazed, and his mouth set in a hungry leer.

"You've been avoiding me," he slurred. "I don't think you understand how stupid that is. If you do this right, you can make a lot of money. A lot. I don't know why I have to teach you, but I guess I have to teach you."

And with that he came at her, swaying forward and seizing her arm while leaning in to kiss her. With his free hand he clumsily groped at her breasts. Although Natalie had been temporarily paralyzed with fear, Miles's hands on her body triggered a reaction. She reflexively pulled back and kicked him in the shin, causing enough pain to force him to pause his attack, giving Natalie the opportunity to shove him aside and sprint through the door. She had the presence of mind to grab her purse as she ran past the bar, continuing out the front door and onto the street. She never looked back and was back in Mobile the next day, her idyllic vision of Key West—my Key West—forever destroyed. And for this, Miles Highgate Jr. would pay. I would see to it.

But with all of those facts alleged in a complaint asserting claims for sexual harassment, battery, and intentional infliction of emotional distress against the hotel and Miles personally, what was the purpose of a futile motion to dismiss? This was the thought I had as I turned onto the Palm Avenue Causeway from North Roosevelt Boulevard, moving steadily at a seven-minute pace. The law firm Miles had hired was based in New York, but had a Miami office. Lawrence, Luckman & Gray, known generally as Lawrence Luckman, was a large general practice firm with a well-regarded merger and acquisition section. Its notoriety, however, came from its litigation department, which had consciously sought to represent the leaders in every industry profitably imperiling American individual and environmental health: cigarette manufacturers, coal mining conglomerates, oil and gas producers, and pharmaceutical companies. All of these, to one degree or another, were besieged by lawsuits threatening their very existence, impelling them to write blank checks to the lawyers defending them, accompanied by one directive: "Win. We won't question the tactics or the cost." Lawrence Luckman was happy to accept the public relations hit that came along with record levels of profits per partner year after year pursuant to these arrangements. Miles Highgate

Jr., was their kind of client, and the Miami office was perfectly situated to wage a war in Key West.

Which is exactly what this was, I suddenly realized. This motion was the first volley in what they were assuring me would be a long, hard fight. The Miami lawyer, a partner named Eva Gutierrez, obviously knew who my father was and undoubtedly knew about me and my exit from Miami. I didn't have a website, but it wouldn't have taken her long to discover that I ran my small legal practice through an office-sharing relationship with a three-person Key West criminal defense firm. For the most part, my practice was actually conducted in cyberspace accessed through my laptop computer. Consistent with her firm's standard practice, I realized, Eva was planning to big-time me, hoping to beat me into submission by filing motion after motion and engaging in protracted and expensive pretrial procedure. Sooner or later, she believed, I would persuade my client to accept a modest settlement rather than continue what would feel like an endless war of attrition. But she didn't know me. I was no longer backing down from a fight.

This thought brought a grim smile to my face as I turned down Whitehead Street and passed the courthouse where the day's skirmish would play out. I wondered if the judge, the Honorable Mark Johnson, would understand how the defense was preparing to do battle and whether he saw the motion for what it was.

As it turned out, he did. I walked into the courtroom for the twenty-minute hearing a little before the scheduled four p.m. start time. I wore a conservatively cut coal-black suit, a stiffly starched white pinpoint Oxford dress shirt, and a modest burgundy silk tie. Heading down the aisle to the counsel tables inside the bar, I saw what I expected at the defense table: Eva, an older man I guessed was a partner from New York, a young, eager-looking

male associate in a tight blue suit and skinny tie, and a paralegal sitting behind the table next to a box presumably filled with
critical documents. A large binder filled with applicable cases and
statutes lay open before Eva on the table, and the New York partner was pulling files from a large leather trial briefcase perched
precariously on the table's edge. The associate held a paper-bound
book of Florida procedural rules for ready access.

I carried a single yellow legal pad on which I had scribbled a
few notes and a blue plastic Paper Mate pen. I casually tossed
both on the plaintiff's table as I turned to greet my adversaries
with what I hoped was a confidently cheerful smile. Eva, a short,
stout woman primly dressed in a navy-blue suit complete with an
American flag lapel pin, grimly introduced me to the others in
her group and abruptly sat down, poring over a case marked with
yellow highlighter. Sitting down at the plaintiff's table, I looked
over at the courtroom deputy standing by the door to the judge's
chambers. He rolled his eyes with a slight shake of the head. That
was a good sign. The judges' deputies often reflect the attitudes of
their assigned judges on particular cases of note.

Right on time, Judge Johnson streamed through the door in his
flowing black robe as the deputy announced, "All rise." The judge
was all business as he took his seat behind the raised bench and
said, "State your appearances and then be seated."

"Jack Girard, on behalf of the plaintiff, Natalie Prudhomme,
Your Honor," I said quickly.

As I anticipated, Eva took a deep breath and began. "My name
is Eva Gutierrez, Judge Johnson. I am a partner in the Miami
office of Lawrence Luckman, an international law firm based in
New York City. This is my New York partner, Neil Swan, and my
Miami associate, Tobin Marshall. Behind me is paralegal Linda
Potter. Collectively we are representing both defendants in this

case. We are here today on our motion to dismiss the plaintiff's scandalous and entirely defective complaint. May I begin?"

She asked this last question as she strode toward the speaker's podium positioned in the center of the room directly before the judge.

Judge Johnson glanced at me and said, "Ms. Gutierrez, I'll save you the trouble. I've read your motion and I've read the complaint. Motion denied. You have ten days to answer. Mr. Swan, I wish you safe travels back to New York."

Mr. Swan's mouth was agape. Eva blurted out, "But . . . but, Judge! You haven't heard my argument! This is highly irregular!"

To which the judge responded, "Ms. Gutierrez, I've ruled. If you utter another word, you will risk contempt. Do you understand me?"

Noticing Eva's red-faced hesitation, he added, "You may answer."

"Yes, Judge."

"Excellent, is there anything else?"

I jumped up to respond, "No, Your Honor."

"Then we are adjourned."

With that, Judge Johnson quickly left the room through the door held open by the deputy, who winked at me as he closed it. I picked up my pad and pen and headed for the aisle, pausing to wave goodbye to the stunned lawyers at the defense table and say, "If you're staying over, Mr. Swan, I would recommend dinner at the A&B Lobster House. Talk soon, Eva."

It wasn't until I raced down three flights of stairs and burst through the doors leading toward Whitehead Street that I threw my head back and howled with laughter. Without question, that was the easiest hearing of my career, and I was still chuckling at the looks on those lawyers' faces as they swallowed the bitter prospect of litigating before a hostile judge when I nearly walked into

Anna Markova, standing resolutely on the sidewalk skirting the parking lot. She wore a simple purple sundress with tiny pink and white flowers. Her arms were folded, but her expression seemed inviting.

"Hello, Jack. I am waiting for you."

CHAPTER TWENTY-ONE

"Anna! Wow. How the heck did you find me here?"

"Pretty simple. I hear through coconut telegraph that you are back in town so I stop by the bar hoping to catch you before it gets busy. The bartender says you are at courthouse doing a lawyer thing. I walk over but I am not sure which room you are in so I wait here."

She paused and looked up at the massive branches off the ancient kapok tree shielding her from the bright late afternoon sun.

"It is a beautiful day, is it not, Jack?"

Thrown by the non sequitur, I mumbled, "Oh yeah. Beautiful. Really."

Pulling myself together and self-consciously aware of the effect her beauty had on me, I said, a little too exuberantly, "Plus, I won!"

No reaction.

"The hearing. The lawyer thing. I won . . . Without actually saying anything . . . It was kind of a big deal."

These last words trailed off quietly as I read the look of incomprehension on her face. But she saved me, as politely as possible.

"I am very happy for you, Jack. You were no doubt impressive, judging by this beautiful suit. Myself, I am most impressed," she said while flashing her most radiant smile.

With the embers of attraction reheating, I could feel myself blushing. I tried to shift to neutral territory before I stupidly said something witty or charming.

"Tracy said you stopped by the bar looking for me the other night. I never got a chance to say goodbye before I left. So I wondered if there was something . . . unfinished from Saturday morning."

Her smile evaporated as she said, "No, nothing unfinished. For you anyway. But I must talk to you. There is something I must say."

Uh-oh. This could be bad in a hundred ways.

Trying to keep my tone light, I said, "Okay. Why don't we go back to the bar and have a drink."

"No, Jack. Not the bar. It is mostly empty now. Could we just sit here on the wall?"

She pointed to the long wall running in front of the old courthouse along Whitehead Street. Glancing down at my suit and at the thigh-high hem of her dress, I suggested, "Why don't we just go over to the Courthouse Deli and sit on the bench? I don't see anyone there yet."

The Courthouse Deli sits directly across the street from the Green Parrot Bar, a famous live music venue in Old Town and a stone's throw from where we were standing. The park bench in front of the deli has become a gathering spot for people who want to hear the music emitting from the Green Parrot's open doors and windows without having to go inside and actually buy a drink. The concept irritated me but was emblematic of the easygoing spirit of Key West. At the moment, there was no music, and the bench had not drawn a crowd.

"Okay, "Anna said. "We go."

And with that she set off in front of me, forcing me against my will to observe her finely shaped legs disappearing into the gentle swaying folds of her dress as she took those long, fluid strides toward the sidewalk.

"Wait for me," I muttered as I hustled up alongside her. I noticed the purposefulness in the set of her jaw in my peripheral vision as we walked along. Neither of us spoke again until we were seated. I put my legal pad on the bench between us, subconsciously creating separation. I started running through possibilities of what this could be about but never got close to what it turned out to be.

Turning to look at me, Anna opened her mouth as if to speak but hesitated, clearly struggling with how to begin. She crossed her legs and clasped her hands on her knee, leaning forward to stare down vacantly at the sidewalk. She took a deep breath, leaned back, and turned to look at me again, her eyes searching my face for something, perhaps some clue as to how I would receive what she had to say.

I tried to help. With a hint of a smile, I said, "Just tell me, Anna. I can handle it, whatever it is."

"This I am sure of, Jack," she said softly. "About me, I am not so sure."

After a moment's pause, she started again, this time focusing her gaze out toward the street and the stream of cars, scooters, and bikes traversing it.

"I think you are aware of how I make money, yes?"

She glanced at me briefly and saw me nod.

"What you might not know is how it works, the business part."

In response to my silence, she pressed ahead.

"Some of my clients pay me a certain amount of money every month. In return, they get access on short notice and a range of . . . services."

"Like a retainer," I said helpfully.

"Yes, Jack. Like retainer for lawyer. Me, I like this arrangement because it gives me a steady income I count on. I buy property around town with this money. I have three houses I rent now."

She said this with a hint of pride. I had to admit I was surprised, although not as surprised as I was about to be.

"Some of these clients pay large amounts, for which they get preferred treatment and more services. Others pay less but get less. You see? I can always say no to any request, no questions asked, but if I do this too often, no more client. Do you understand?"

"Yep. I think I've got it."

She shifted on the bench and looked at me straight in the eye as she said, "One of these clients is your father, Jack."

I recoiled as though she had slapped me. I had never imagined the Duke in this context and was unable to actually see him in it. Anna watched me process the information, her face betraying no emotion as she waited, very likely expecting the worst. Is this why we were sitting in a public place? Were her expectations of men—of me—so low that she anticipated violence, in word if not in action? I thought back to our encounter at the bar Friday night and her reaction to my intervention with the Navy pilots. She was never afraid, certain that she could handle whatever came next—Jack or no Jack. Now, looking at her impassive face, her blue eyes frozen like glacier ice, I found myself reflecting on her choices rather than mine. What had been a business proposition for her no longer was. She had made a decision and was here to see it through.

Instead of expressing the outrage she expected, I asked, in the softest tone I could muster, "Why are you telling me this, Anna? What's changed?"

Turning back to look out over the street, she considered her response before saying, "I think more than one thing, Jack. I would like now to tell you the story, which is really not so much."

Shifting again to look at me, her natural seduction radiating, she asked, "May I do this, Jack?"

"I've got nowhere else to be, Anna."

I loosened my tie and undid the top button of my shirt.

"Please," I said, gesturing for her to proceed.

"Okay." Another pause and then, "About one year ago, I got a call on my cell phone from a man identifying himself as Duke Girard. I do not know this name and ask how he gets my number. Perhaps this is mistake. He laughs at this and tells me it is no mistake and my number is not so hard to get as I might think. We begin to talk but I am wary. This is 305 number he is calling from and it could be Monroe County sting operation. He senses I am uneasy and tells me to hang up and google Duke Girard. He says if I am interested in easy business proposition, I should call the number I find there and ask for him and I will be connected. So I do this. Why not? There is no harm in finding out what he wants."

With this she glanced over at me but discovered that I was now the one betraying no emotion. My mind was working hard, trying to jump ahead, but I remained still, determined to stay in the moment.

She continued. "When I call, a secretary puts me through and there he is again. I think he's smiling, knowing I would do this."

She looked at me expectantly.

"He was definitely smiling and he definitely knew you would call, Anna. Predicting people is his thing." I allowed myself a grim chuckle as I said this. "Go on."

"He says he wants to pay me $2,000 a month to be on call for him. For me, this is not much money so it is my turn to smile as I tell him there is not much he can get for this small amount. I am preparing to hang up when he says I am not understanding his request. He says he is not hiring me for sex work. He asks me if I know the bar called Billy & Bob's. I say yes, and he asks me if I know the new owner, a young man named Jack Girard."

She stopped to look at me again, something like embarrassment creeping into her expression. With no interruption from me, she pressed ahead.

"Well, I tell him I don't know Jack Girard but I ask if he's related because of the last name. He says it is his son and he simply wants someone he can trust to keep secrets and not to keep records to look in on his son from time to time. He wants to know how he is doing but does not want his son to know he is doing this. I do not ask why and—I'm sorry, Jack—I do not care because this is really easy money. So this is how it begins."

"*Begins*? I'd like to know, Anna. Was there ever sex involved?" My voice was a little strained.

"No, Jack, there never was. Of course, I knew you would want to know this and I am grateful you did not ask until now. But this would have been . . . available . . . at the beginning if he asks for it, but he never does. Now, it would not be available. This is one thing that has changed."

I felt a trace of tenderness in her tone as she reached out to touch my hand but thought better of it and pulled back.

"What else has changed, Anna?" I asked as coolly as I could.

"Well, Jack, I begin to think about things after I leave you Saturday morning. You know, I think that I recognize the number calling in on your cell phone."

Actually, I hadn't thought about that at all, hungover and stressed as I was. But I said nothing, nodding for her to continue.

"Anyway, I understand from conversation that your mother takes her own life. I do not think your father knows I am in the room, listening. After leaving I think about the last week and it all seems strange, the timing. This is what I am here to tell you. I don't understand it, but maybe you do."

She paused for a moment, visibly gathering her thoughts so she could communicate them sensibly. I took the moment to ask, "So when did you last speak to the Duke?"

"It is last Saturday. In the afternoon. He says you're going to Miami and asks if I have any trouble with you Friday night."

"Trouble? What do you mean?"

I wasn't following this.

"This is the thing, Jack. After talking to him once or twice a month, suddenly last week he's calling me every day. He wants to be sure you are in Key West. He asks me to try to . . . to be friends with you. This is not working with my schedule until Friday, however. I do not tell him this. He believes I am seeing you each day. Then, on Friday, he calls to say he wants me to see you and would like it if you get very drunk. I do not understand this, but the rest you know. I am now thinking he wants you to be hungover, possibly not thinking clearly, when he calls you."

And he wanted me drunk or hungover for the next three days, I thought to myself. I was now thinking clearly.

"Anna, when did he first call you last week asking for you to try to . . . make friends with me?"

Anna looked down at her hands in her lap as she tried to remember. Her long fingers were tipped in blood-red polish.

"It is the Saturday before," she announced at last. "He says he is on business trip and needs to know if you have plans to go anywhere, Miami for instance. He says it is best if you stay in Key West."

It was so like the Duke to believe I was always itching to get out of Key West. Little did he know I had no plans to ever leave until he called me. But why did he care?

"Where was he when he called you, Anna? Did he say?"

"In New York. He is giving a speech there."

"New York?" I mused out loud. Gina Martelli's hometown. On the weekend she disappeared.

"I think I've got it, Anna. Thank you."

My tone was subdued, but my mind was racing, fitting puzzle pieces in their places to form a grotesque image in which I was a hapless part. No more. That picture was going to change. There was peace in the certainty of my conviction.

Evidently noticing the menacing cast to my expression, Anna broke through, saying, "I would not like to be the person you're thinking of now, Jack. I will go."

As she stood, I reached out and took her hand, gently pulling her back onto the bench. I had to know.

"So Friday night was just business, Anna?"

Looking at me intently, I noticed wetness in the corners of her eyes.

"Yes, Jack, it begins this way. But as we go on drinking—too much, for both of us—I begin to tell you things, parts of my life that have brought me shame. But you do not pull away. You draw closer to me and tell me things, kind things no man has said. I know you do not remember this, but I do. I cannot forget. I cannot hurt this man. I tell your father I am through with arrangement when he calls on Saturday. He laughs and says it is okay. The job is done."

"Actually, Anna, it isn't."

After a pause for reflection, I added, "But no matter what happens, you and I are friends."

And then I leaned in to kiss her softly. She responded, without resistance.

CHAPTER TWENTY-TWO

I was comfortable, even exhilarated, traveling southeast across Biscayne Bay at thirty knots on a brisk cloudless night under a bright half-moon. I was at the helm of the Intrepid, the boat of my youth. *Betty's Boys*. Betty herself was present, reduced to ashes in a thick plastic ziplock bag stowed in a compartment at my feet. The Duke stood next to me, leaning on the bench seat behind us, eyes fixed forward toward the twinkling lights on the southern end of Key Biscayne. I was certain I could find my way on my own, having made the trip to Fowey Light in the dark many times, but the Duke had insisted we plot the course on his new Fortuno GPS/Fishfinder, not trusting my memory.

Our meeting on the dock at Rockerman Road had been uneasy. I had called on Friday afternoon to say I had been tied up and would meet him at the boat. In the meantime, I had also called my grandparents. No answer; nothing but voicemail. Which made it impossible not to stop at the Old Cutler mansion as I retraced my steps toward Rockerman Road.

. . .

As I pulled in on the long crushed-shell driveway, I was aware of the noise the Jeep created as it crunched along toward the circle before the entrance to the main house in the dark, early hours of the morning. Stepping out, this familiar place seemed foreign; I became aware of the troop of green parrots noisily working seeds in the royal poinciana trees surrounding the house. I felt cold. There was nothing to remind me of the days when I laughed running around these grounds, chasing Bobby as we played two-man tag before falling, hot but happy, into the pool facing the bay. As I approached the massive and ancient oak door, prepared to knock using the painted cast-iron knocker we once raced to reach first, I was surprised when the door swung open. My grandfather, Magnus Donovan, stout and steely-eyed, his thick white hair swept back from his tanned and unlined forehead, stood in the doorway, as though he had heard me coming.

"Jack. Such a surprise after all this time."

Eyeing my attire, he added, "Given the time, you must be going fishing."

My grandfather was naturally an early riser and was used to early-morning forays on the water behind his house.

"Hello, Gramps. I wish we had spoken sooner."

He gave no indication that he would be inviting me in, so I got right to the point as I stepped closer, wondering if he would back up if I kept pressing forward.

"I wanted to tell you something important. To me, anyway. I think you've been too hard on your daughter. You, God—no one—should judge her based on what you think went down at the end. She didn't want to die. But she was willing to. She was. I'm not going to try to change anything you think, but I wanted you to know that one thing."

His expression was unchanged, inscrutable. He wasn't backing up.

"What are you saying, Jack? Don't speak in riddles. Are you saying Betty didn't commit suicide?"

"That's not what I'm saying. I'm saying she didn't die voluntarily. There was more to it. I think you should have given her more credit, but then that was hard for you, I know."

"Jack, excuse my language, but don't fuck with me. Did someone kill Betty? Do you know something? If you don't, please leave. I can't stand here looking at you, her spitting image, and see anything but a ghost."

"I do know something, Gramps. I just don't know all of it, but I think you'll know the truth, the actual truth, very soon. I just wanted to tell you that. And that I love you."

He wasn't ready for that. He stammered and started to speak, but I turned and walked back to the Jeep, firing up the engine and pulling ahead in the driveway as my mother's father closed the door. I'd said what I came to say.

· · ·

When I finally arrived at the dock, the Duke was standing impatiently next to his new Contender in a heavy orange Helly Hansen foul weather jacket and matching pants. He resembled a large traffic cone as I approached until he raised his arm to look at his watch reproachfully. It was sixty-eight degrees and breezy, but that looked like a lot of foul weather gear for the conditions. Lots of large pockets. I was wearing jeans, a long-sleeved tee shirt, and my blue Pelagic windbreaker, presently unzipped. As I drew closer, he turned to board the Contender, but I said, "Let's take the Intrepid. For old times' sake. I'll drive."

He stopped, turned, and looked at me for several long seconds before saying, "Okay, Jack. Give me a minute. We'll need the guest of honor."

With that, he hopped on board the Contender and disappeared inside the forward compartment, returning after several minutes with the plastic bag containing my mother's ashes and a two-foot weather-proof gear bag. What might he have in there, I wondered? I boarded the Intrepid and did a quick visual inspection. With mock solemnity, the Duke asked, "Permission to come aboard, Captain?"

"Granted," I said, refusing to acknowledge the sarcasm. "Let me help with those," I added, pointing at the bags.

The Duke handed me the ashes, but not the gear bag as he stepped up on the gunwale and jumped into the boat. I stowed the ashes beneath the helm, and the Duke put the bag down gently at the foot of the console where he would be riding. After the initial sparring about the course to Fowey Light, I started the engines, fired up the GPS, and set the coordinates for the trip. There was nothing left to do but cast off. I had no particular thought as we did so; the Rubicon had been crossed, my fate was my own.

As we approached the southern end of Key Biscayne from the northwest, I decided to change course slightly, turning closer to shore, easing back on the throttles and proceeding through the Cape Florida Channel to the Atlantic Ocean. Judging by the noise they made, the GPS and the Duke would have much preferred I continue farther south and use the well-marked and partially dredged Biscayne Channel, but I was the captain and I knew the way through the shoals.

In the darkness, I could only guess at the entrance to No Name Harbor, the small tree-lined cove carved into the western edge of Key Biscayne where my family spent many an enjoyable day at anchor in this very boat, swimming, diving, and playing in the calm, emerald-hued water. There was a time, not in my memory alone, when the four Girards comprised a unified whole, like a single organism with disparate qualities in delicate balance. Now, the remaining two proceeded alone—despite being separated by a mere twelve inches—toward a common destination. What each would find there was all that was left to be revealed.

Safely through to the ocean side with the Fowey Light shining brightly seven miles to the south, I punched the throttles forward, now eager to complete the journey. I felt the Duke watching me intently as the Intrepid gracefully rose on plane, effortlessly handling the one- to two-foot seas. We had barely spoken since leaving the dock, aided in our preference for silence by the sound of the engines and the wind sweeping through the cockpit. But I could sense the Duke formulating a speech, or at least the outline of one, designed to elicit information he wasn't sure I had. I think he was determining whether my apparent lack of anxiety reflected ignorance or resolve. He was leaning toward ignorance, underestimating me to the last.

As we came within a half-mile of the lighthouse, its 110-foot triangular form loomed as a solid dark shape in the shadow of the light and the half-moon above us. A silvery white glow shimmered on the wave crests ahead. Closing within a hundred yards, I noticed on the fishfinder that we had passed the reef line and were over a sandy bottom. Cutting back to idle speed, I turned into the wind and the Duke nimbly hopped forward to drop the anchor in seventeen feet of water without being told. We had done this before. With the anchor secure, I cut the engines, and we found ourselves in the eerie near-silence you can only experience on the water at night. Waves lapped against the hull, and a light breeze rustled through the boat. As the Duke stepped back into the cockpit, he looked at his watch and said, "Twenty minutes until sunrise. How do you want to kill the time, Jack?"

I detected a mirthless smile on his face in the gloom. He leaned over and reached toward the gear bag at his feet. I jumped upright at the helm and turned to face him squarely. Quickly unzipping the bag, he pulled out a small steel thermos and a short sleeve of mini disposable espresso cups, saying, "Marta insisted on sending along her best Cuban coffee. She packed a bottle of champagne also, for later."

I immediately relaxed, but not before the Duke noticed the sudden tension. Before he could speak, I said, "Coffee would be perfect. Let's move to the stern."

I stepped out and turned toward the rear, as though that had been my intention all along. I sat on the port gunwale, the hulking form of the lighthouse seventy yards to my back. The Duke followed, handing me the thermos and cups before returning to the cockpit to pick up his bag, quickly zipping it while his back was turned to me. But not before I saw him fumbling around inside it. Turning, he said, "I guess I don't need this jacket anymore. It will warm right up when the sun rises."

"Yep. That's how it works, Dad."

Ignoring me, the Duke took off the jacket and tossed it on the bench seat. Carrying the bag, he carefully stepped to the rear and seated himself opposite me on the starboard gunwale, facing the lighthouse. He was wearing a white knit sweater along with the orange pants and his customary deck shoes. He put the gear bag between his feet, stretched his arms outward, and took a deep breath of the slightly humid, salty air.

"Many memories here, Jack. Many good times. Seeing you sitting there, I can't help but think of your brother, the times we had here, just the two of us."

I couldn't quite see the expression on his face as he surveyed the ocean behind the boat in the direction of the low-wattage glow that would soon be the horizon, as yet indistinct. He added in a low tone, as if to himself, "My, how you loved the water."

I knew he wasn't talking to me.

Breaking the spell, I got up to hand him a steaming cup of Marta's coffee. Taking a sip, he said, "Somehow it always tastes better out here."

"I agree with you there," I replied as I sat down again. "I'd forgotten things like that."

I could feel the Duke's eyes on me in the ensuing silence. I sipped my coffee and wondered what he was thinking. I didn't have to wait long to find out.

"Jack, I'm not going to insult you by asking you first. I know you talked to Steve Amos, and I know you talked to the DEA. You didn't tell me about either conversation. That forces me to consider who else you might have talked to and what conclusions you might have drawn. However I work it, I can't think of an acceptable reason for your silence."

So he wanted to do this here, on this day and in this place. Personally, I would have preferred to wait, but I could see the advantages from his point of view. We were alone with little risk of interruption or observation. He felt in control of the situation despite being on the smaller boat against his preference. He believed he knew me and was comfortable with the outcome of each scenario he had undoubtedly worked through in his mind. I edged forward on the gunwale, placing more weight on my feet. Fuck it. I had thought about things, too.

"Well, it could be—Dad—that I'm just letting it go. Mom really did kill herself because her life didn't turn out the way she hoped. It's a tragedy, but that's all it is."

Pausing, I noticed that the Duke had put his coffee in the adjacent cup-holder, freeing his hands, which were now placed lightly on his knees. His face was inscrutable in the dim radiance of the lighthouse, although I could see his white teeth in what must have been a smile.

"But I won't insult you with bullshit," I continued. "I know you killed Gina Martelli two weeks ago. Gina Martelli. A name I had to discover on my own. A name you didn't share while you were pointing me at Julio Guzman. You remember . . . Dad. Your wife's lover. The one whose portrait you didn't recognize."

Of course, I was only ninety percent sure; it was a purely circumstantial conclusion. But the Duke's reaction would tell the tale. It was already telling that he let me complete that speech without interrupting in angry denial. He sat quietly, not moving, for several seconds. This was a scenario he had considered and he was deciding how it should run. He spoke, almost conversationally.

"It could have been so easy, Jack. The divorce could have been painless. The money was already split. The affair with Guzman? Pretty understandable. An attractive, powerful man. These things happen. Blah, blah, blah. My dignity comes out of it unmarked."

He paused.

"But a woman?!!! Abso-fucking-lutely impossible. Not my wife. No fucking way. I would be a laughingstock. Every judge, every defense lawyer . . . shit, everyone that works for me would be snickering behind my back, mocking me, telling their little jokes. That kind of shit happens to other sorry fucks. Not the Duke!"

His face was becoming visible in the emerging light. The sun had not reached the horizon, but a yellow-white gleam signaled its impending arrival. The Duke's eyes were wide, the black irises magnified by the dimness. His mouth hung open, prepared to speak but searching for the words. At last he said, "At least you can understand this, can't you, Jack?"

There was a plaintive tone in his voice that was uncharacteristic.

I was riveted, careful not to move. Now that we were here, there was more I needed to know.

"Oh, I understand perfectly. But why go after Guzman? That sort of backfired."

"Because I definitely wanted to hurt him. He took what was mine and needed to pay. It was a great way to tie things up, no matter what you did. If you went to the cops with it, I would be shielded and, at the worst, maybe his drug business would be exposed. If you took a more aggressive—let's say tactical— approach to the problem, so much the better. But I didn't think you would actually talk to him. Which I now know you did. It's the only way you could have found out about the lesbo."

Ignoring the disparaging term, I asked quietly, hoping to keep him in rhythm, "How did you work it with Mom?"

He barked out a laugh and said, "That part was easy. When I saw Betty that night, she knew the second I walked in the door it was over. I hadn't thought about much else since she told me about it, and I don't think she'd ever seen death looking back at her until she saw me. I've had that effect before. I guess she was a little scared, but not so much that she couldn't make love to her own husband, the way it was intended! She didn't fight me, Jack."

He raped her, confirming my worst fear. His own wife. My mother. I felt my stomach turning and my rage rising. I had to stay calm. The sun was just breaking through off the stem of the boat, the orange edge glowing and casting a purple and yellow halo into the eastern sky.

"What about the note? And the pills?"

"Look, Jack, she knew she was going to die that night, one way or another. I was going to throw her off the balcony if I had to. I gave her a choice and she made the right one. I didn't care about the note as long as she didn't say anything stupid."

No, I thought. *It wasn't stupid. It was brilliant.*

Out loud, I said, "What now?"

I was thinking hard about how to attack and subdue him. The gentle rocking of the boat made any straight-line movement difficult.

"Well, Son, as you know, the thing that separates humans from other animals is the will to power. And the thing that separates one man from another is the power of his will. My will is very powerful."

As he was saying this, he slowly leaned forward and reached down toward his gear bag. He never took his eyes off me as he unzipped the bag, reached in, and pulled out a lethal-looking handgun I couldn't identify. Damn it! I was afraid that's what was in there with the coffee thermos. I guessed there would be no champagne.

"You don't seem surprised, Jack. That's interesting."

He held the gun in two hands. It was pointed at the center of my chest. I was judging the time it would take to lunge forward and knock him over backward into the water. Longer than his reaction time, I feared; his finger was on the trigger.

"But what we're going to do is what we came out here to do. We're going to return your mother to the sea. You and I will come to some resolution afterward. Sounds like a plan?"

"You're the one with the gun."

"Yes. And don't test my willingness to use it. There's a way out of this, Jack. But first things first."

With that he stood up, the first rays of the rising sun illuminating his face and chest, causing him to squint as he looked past me toward the lighthouse. There was a hint of surprise in his eyes in the moment I saw the small crimson circle appear on his chest just below his left shoulder, the crack of a rifle shot following near-simultaneously. The force of the blow caused the Duke to stumble backward and to his left, catapulting him over the gunwale and into the water. Crouching down, I peered toward the lighthouse and saw a figure on the planked wooden service platform ten feet off the surface. In the still-dim light I could just make out the rifle pointing skyward, the man holding it facing away from me, watching the progress of a large, deep-vee hulled racing boat roaring toward the lighthouse from the south. As he turned back to spot the Duke, the emerging light glinted off the metallic clip holding back his thick black hair. This was Guzman's driver, I was sure. What were his plans for me? I considered crawling forward and starting the engines, but I wasn't sure where the Duke was, and we were still at anchor. I saw the driver looking through the scope of his rifle trying to spot the Duke, who was apparently blocked by the boat.

Just then, the power boat arrived at the platform, its skilled operator holding it steadily just off the lighthouse pilings. *"Vamos ahora, muchacho,"* he shouted, clearly unsure how long he could hold his position. The driver hesitated momentarily before reaching down and unrolling a rope ladder that had been stowed on the platform. Throwing the rifle into the boat, he began his descent. Spotting me watching, he waved once and yelled, *"Buena suerte,* Jack," followed by a high-pitched laugh. He jumped into the boat, detached the ladder, pulled it in, and they were off—quickly turning away from the lighthouse and heading into the sunrise toward the Bahamas beyond.

I leaped up and across to the starboard side of the boat where I saw the Duke floating twenty yards away and to the rear, his right arm treading against the current, his left arm still.

When he saw me, he called, "Okay, Jack, come and get me. I can't swim against this current." His voice was weak and raspy.

Noticing my hesitation, he added, "The gun is gone, Jack. I dropped it. I can't use my left arm. I think you can handle me. If you leave me here, you'll be the only suspect in my death. So let's go. I'm getting sleepy."

At that, I reached into the pocket of my windbreaker and pulled out the mini micro-stick voice-activated recorder I had picked up at a spy store in downtown Miami the day before. I hit the REWIND button and then PLAY. The Duke's voice emitted from the tiny speaker, ". . . I was going to throw her off the balcony . . ."

"Fuck that, Jack. It's not admissible against me."

His voice trailed off as he mumbled something more.

"Maybe, maybe not. But it'll keep me out of jail, wouldn't you say?"

And then he vanished, right before my eyes. There was a violent churning in the water as a large black form breached the surface and plunged back, creating a surface wake as it moved with the current toward the deeper water to the east. El Toro. The shark had been attracted by the blood and couldn't discern precisely what creature this was in the still-dark water. I stood paralyzed, staring eastward, waiting for the Duke to resurface somewhere.

Finally, after about twenty seconds, the Duke's head popped up another hundred feet from the boat. I turned and leaped to the helm, starting the engines and shifting into forward drive to create slack in the anchor line. I jumped onto the bow as the boat idled ahead and pulled up the anchor in a frenzied rush. Back at the wheel in the cockpit, I turned the boat around and edged the throttles forward. Only then, as I saw the Duke's right arm waving in the distance, did I think of what I was doing. The Duke saw me coming, now seventy feet away. Feeling a burst of adrenaline, he shouted, "Good, Jack, come and get me. The shark got a piece of my leg. You've got to hurry. He's still circling."

When sharks attack large prey, they inflict an initial forceful bite and then depart to avoid possible injury from the thrashing victim. They circle the area and wait for the victim to bleed out and stop moving. The Duke knew that. So did I.

As I closed to within twenty feet, the Duke said, weaker now, "Okay, Jack. Put it in neutral and throw me a line."

I didn't do as he asked. Instead, I veered slightly to port, heading due east toward the horizon. As I passed the Duke—ten feet to starboard—I glanced briefly at his shocked expression.

"What are you doing, Jack? You can't leave me! Jack!"

Now ten feet astern, shock turned to anger.

"Fuck this, Jack! Get back here! This is bullshit!"

His voice was now muffled by the low rumble of the boat's engines. He was pleading.

"Please, Jack. Come . . . back."

Before his voice became indistinct, did I hear him say, "I'm sorry, Jack"? Does it matter one way or the other? My mind still toys with that one. At the time, the possibility made me turn to look. He was gone.

I continued eastward for what must have been a few minutes, seemingly unable to move. My hands gripped the wheel so tightly I lost feeling. My jaw clenched to the point of pain. Finally, taking deep breaths, I regained control of myself. In the moment, I could think of only one thing to do before declaring "mayday" on VHF Channel 16 and waiting for the Coast Guard or police to arrive. I pulled my mother's ashes from the compartment beneath the helm and returned to the stern of the boat. I unzipped the bag and carefully poured the contents into the sea, struck by the irony of the last remnants of Betty and the Duke mixing and drifting toward the Gulf Stream together on this dazzlingly clear new day. I thought about my brother as the ashes dispersed and eventually disappeared.

"Farewell," was all I could muster.

Watching the sun continue to rise, I was mesmerized by the water—imagining the blood flowing through my veins—as it changed from black to the deepest indigo to inky blue. It was a start.

BOOK CLUB DISCUSSION QUESTIONS

1. Jack wrestles with the pliability of the past and desperately wants to accurately describe the events he experienced. Does he succeed? Do you think this type of retrospection matters?

2. Did you conclude that the Duke was a truly evil person? What was the deciding factor? Did you find any redeeming factors?

3. Did Bobby die because he believed his life had become worthless or because he felt helpless to cope in the world his father controlled? Could he have distinguished those? In other words, was the Duke to blame, as Jack believed, or did Bobby give up?

4. Could Betty have saved Bobby had she understood his dilemma?

5. How do you think Jack handled the professional ruin the Duke forced on him?

6. Do you think that Jack could have done more to help his brother and his mother better understand themselves?

7. Jack sought redemption, possibly subconsciously. Did he achieve it? Did your view of this change with the choice he made at the end?

8. Have you ever known someone with the Duke's ultra-rigid belief in their own version of "reality"?

9. What do you predict for Jack when he goes home to Key West? Do you think he will return to Miami?

10. What advice would you give to Jack?